Look what people are saying about Jill Shalvis...

"Riveting suspense laced with humor and heart is her hallmark and Jill Shalvis always delivers."
—*USA TODAY* bestselling author Donna Kauffman

"For those of you who haven't read Jill Shalvis, you are really missing out."
—*In the Library Reviews*

"Jill Shalvis displays the soul of a poet with her deft pen, creating a powerful atmosphere."
—*WordWeaving*

"Jill Shalvis is a breath of fresh air on a hot, humid night."
—*thereadersconnection.com*

"Jill Shalvis has the incredible talent of creating characters who are intelligent, quick-witted, and gorgeously sexy, all the while giving them just the right amount of weakness to keep them from being unrealistically perfect."
—*Romance Junkies*

Blaze™

Dear Reader,

I'm drawn to action-adventure movies, and if they have a romance in them, well then, that's just icing on the cake. So it seemed like a logical decision to try my hand at writing one, romance included, of course—an adrenaline-fueled, seriously *sexy* romance. Once I'd found my hero, JT Hawk, it was obvious I couldn't write his story any other way....

So I'd like you to meet Hawk and Abby, fellow ATF agents on the run for their very lives. In the beginning, they irritate—and arouse—the hell out of each other. But danger has a way of bringing out the best in people. And the best between Hawk and Abby is very, *very* good....

Happy reading on this one! And as always, I'd love to hear what you think. You can find me on the Web, along with my daily blog about my own wacky adventures, at www.jillshalvis.com.

Enjoy,

Jill Shalvis

JILL SHALVIS
Shadow Hawk

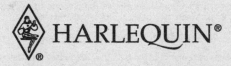

HARLEQUIN®

TORONTO • NEW YORK • LONDON
AMSTERDAM • PARIS • SYDNEY • HAMBURG
STOCKHOLM • ATHENS • TOKYO • MILAN • MADRID
PRAGUE • WARSAW • BUDAPEST • AUCKLAND

ISBN-13: 978-0-373-79333-4
ISBN-10:   0-373-79333-2

SHADOW HAWK

www.eHarlequin.com

Printed in U.S.A.

ABOUT THE AUTHOR

USA TODAY bestselling author Jill Shalvis has written over three dozen romances for Harlequin Books, Penguin and Kensington Publishing. Look for her stories wherever books are sold, and come visit her on the Web, www.jillshalvis.com, where she keeps a daily blog of all her adventures.

Don't miss any of our special offers. Write to us at the following address for information on our newest releases.

Harlequin Reader Service
U.S.: 3010 Walden Ave., P.O. Box 1325, Buffalo, NY 14269
Canadian: P.O. Box 609, Fort Erie, Ont. L2A 5X3

Being a writer can be lonely.
Thankfully, I have a support group.
Thanks to Steph for the sanity lunches.
Thanks to Laurie for the sweet enthusiasm.
And thanks to Gena for...well, everything.
Couldn't have done this one without you.

Prologue

Cheyenne, Wyoming
Regional ATF offices

SHE WAS ALL LEG, and Conner Hawk was most definitely a leg man. Hell, he was also a T&A man, but Abigail Wells, fellow ATF agent and communications expert, not to mention all around hot chick, was so well put together she could have made him a certified elbow man.

Too bad she hated his guts.

She walked—strolled—across the Bureau of Alcohol, Tobacco and Firearms' office, her soft skirt clinging to her thighs with every graceful swing of her hips. Her blazer hid her torso from view, but he knew she had it going on beneath that as well. Her honey-colored hair was pulled up in some complicated do that screamed On Top Of Her World.

As if she'd read the direction his thoughts had traveled, Abigail glanced over at him, those bee-stung lips flipping her smile upside down, her eyes going from work-mode to pissy-female mode.

Oh yeah, *there* was the frown, the one she'd been

giving him ever since the day she joined the team six months ago. She'd come from the Seattle office, where she'd worked in the field. He tried to imagine her wearing an ATF flak jacket, guarding his six, and was halfway lost in that fun fantasy when she spoke.

"You." This in a tone that suggested he could, and should, go to hell.

"Me," he agreed, surprised that she'd even given him that one word. She usually avoided talking directly to him, as if he carried some new infectious disease.

Odd, since to everyone else she'd been personable, even sweet and kind. It made that steely backbone of hers so surprising. When she decided to dig her heels into something, watch out. He'd seen it over and over, people so shocked by the unexpected toughness that this pleasant, melodious little thing exhibited that she got whatever she wanted. She must have been a hell of a force out in the field, probably underestimated by every single scum of the earth who'd come across her, but here in Cheyenne she'd stayed behind the scenes.

"You're late," she said in a school-principal-to-errant-student tone.

Oh yeah, now *there* was a fantasy…. He pulled out his cell phone and looked at the digital readout. Two minutes. He was two minutes late, and that was because someone had taken his parking spot. And he might have explained that to her if she hadn't been giving him the look that people gave their shoe when they stepped on dog shit.

Even as he thought it, her nose slightly wrinkled.

Yeah. In her eyes—which were an amazing drown-in-me blue—he was about equal to dog shit. Nice to know.

"We're wanted in Tibbs's office," Abigail said.

We? Well, *that* was a new term. Hawk dutifully followed her into their supervisor's office, his gaze slipping down that stiff spine to her spectacular ass. Attitude or not, she looked good enough to nibble on. A little sweet, a little hot…nice combo—

Whoa. She'd suddenly stopped, forcing him to put his hands on her hips rather than plow her over.

Clearly hating even that small contact, she jerked free and sent him a look that said go-directly-to-hell-without-passing-Go.

Right. Hands off. Maybe he should write that down somewhere.

"Any news on the rifles?" she asked.

Great. The absolute last thing he wanted to talk about. The rifles. Everyone had heard about the 350 confiscated rifles, which had gone missing from ATF storage before they could be melted down. Stolen, from beneath their noses.

His nose.

She was asking, of course, because he'd been the agent on the raid, the one who'd brought the weapons in. He had no idea how they'd gone missing, but he knew why. They had a mole and Hawk was getting too close.

"No. No news."

"I see." And with one last cool glance, she knocked on Tibbs's door.

I see? What the hell did that mean? Before he could ask, Tibbs called out for them to enter.

Their supervisor stood behind his desk, which didn't make that much of a difference since he was maybe five foot four and nearly as round as he was tall. The balding man shoved his glasses higher on his prominent nose. "We got a tip on the bombers," he said in that Alabama drawl of his.

Hawk had been working on the Kiddie Bombers for the past two years. Some asshole, or group of assholes, was teaching teenagers how to put together bombs, then using the explosives to terrorize big corporations into paying millions of dollars. Twelve kids had died so far, eight of them under the age of eighteen, and the ATF wanted the bomb-makers and their knowledge off the streets.

Hawk wanted that, too, and also the man running the Kiddie Bombers. Eighteen months ago he'd nearly caught him in a raid on a downtown warehouse. In the pitch-black, on the hard concrete floor, they'd fought. Hawk had wrestled a gun from his hand, managing to shoot him before being tackled by another Kiddie Bomber.

Hawk had escaped with his life intact, thanks to his partner, Logan, and given that the gang had gone quiet after that night, it had been assumed that the Kiddie Bombers' leader had died from his gunshot wound.

But a year ago, the Kiddie Bombers had popped back onto the radar, pulling off two huge jobs with weapons that had been previously confiscated by the ATF.

Hawk had his suspicions, mostly because there was only one person who could be linked to all the raids—Elliot Gaines. But that was so crazy wild, so out there, he'd kept it to himself, except for Logan. What he hadn't kept to himself was his vow to get the Kiddie Bombers' leader.

In the past month alone, Hawk and Logan had confiscated two huge warehouses full of ammo and other supplies. But not a single suspect. "Tip?" he asked Tibbs.

"Suspicious activity, rumored arsenal. Orders came down from Gaines on this."

Elliot Gaines was the regional head. Or, as some put it, God. Word had spread that the Almighty was tired of the delays, tired of the false leads and *really* tired of the ATF looking like idiots.

"You're both heading out." Tibbs tossed a full file on his desk for them to read. "Bullet City."

Northern Wyoming, approximately four-and-a-half hours from Nowhere, U.S.A. Yeah, made sense to Hawk. Isolated. Cold, which was good for the materials the bombers used. And, oh yeah, isolated. Great.

"Word is tonight's the night they're testing some new product," Tibbs drawled. "We'll need to catch them in the middle of their private fireworks show."

That worked for Hawk. He picked up the file and flipped through it, reading about the barn that'd been found loaded to the gills with incriminating equipment, complete with an elusive owner they hadn't been able to pin down.

Abby shifted closer to read over Hawk's shoulder,

making him extremely aware of her tension as it crackled through the air like static electricity.

"You've got two hours," Tibbs told them. "You fly out together."

"Together?" Abby repeated, her voice actually cracking.

Surprised at the unexpected chink in her armor, Hawk looked at her.

"You'll run the show from the van, Abby," Tibbs said. "And Hawk from the field. There'll be a team in place."

Abby blinked. "But…"

Both men eyed her as two high splotches of color marked her cheeks. Interesting, Hawk thought. She was usually cool as ice. So what had her riled up? Him? Because she sure as hell got to him. He couldn't help it, beneath her veneer there was just something about her, something…special. Sure, he wanted to do wicked things to her body and vice versa, but that alone wouldn't have kept him on edge around her for six months. "Don't worry," he told her. "I've done this once or twice before."

"Ha." But her brow puckered, her kiss-me-mouth tightened.

Normally this would make him wonder how long he'd have to kiss her before she softened for him, but not now. "What is it? You don't trust me out there?"

"Hawk," Tibbs said quietly.

He heard the warning in his boss's voice, but he didn't care. "No, I think it's time, past time, that we get this out in the open. I want to know, Abby. What exactly is your problem with me?"

"Nothing." She hit him with those baby blues, which were suddenly void of any emotion whatsoever. "There's no problem at all."

Bullshit. But hell if he was going to keep bashing his head against a brick wall. "Okay, then. Fine."

"Fine." She gestured to the file in his hands as she gathered her control around her like a cloak. "Flight's at two." She said this evenly, back to being as cool as a cucumber. In a freezer. In Antarctica. "Be late and I leave without you."

1

Later that night
Twenty-five miles outside of
Bullet City, Wyoming

ABBY ENTERED THE COMMUNICATIONS van, and the men stopped talking. Typical. Men complained that women were the difficult gender, but it seemed to her the penis-carrying half were far more thorny.

Not to mention downright problematic.

Not that she cared, because when it came to personal relationships, she'd given them up. A fact that made her life much simpler.

Sliding the door shut behind her, she shivered. Late fall in the high altitude Bighorn Mountains meant that razor-sharp air cut right through her, layers and all. As she rubbed her frozen hands together, her gaze inadvertently locked on Hawk, who had his long-sleeved black shirt open and the matching T-shirt beneath it shoved up so that he could get wired.

He stood there, six feet two inches of solid badass complete with a wicked, mischievous grin, topped with warm, chocolate eyes that could melt or freeze on a dime. From beneath the sleeve of his T-shirt peeked the very edge of the tattoo on his bicep, which she knew was a hawk.

The women in the office practically swooned at it, every time.

But not Abby. Nope, she was made of firmer stuff.

There was a four-inch scar, old and nearly faded, along his left side between two ribs, and another puckered scar above his left pec. The first was a knife wound, the second a bullet hole. She could also see his smooth, sleek flesh pressed taut to hard, rippled sinew. One long, lean muscle, not an ounce of extra on him.

Whew. Had she been cold only a moment before? Because suddenly, she was starting to sweat. She cursed her 20/20 vision.

Maybe she wasn't made of firmer stuff after all…. But regardless, she was over men. *So* over men. And seeing that she'd become so enlightened…she blew out a breath and moved to her communications station.

Where for the first time, she hesitated. That in itself pissed her off. So a year ago she'd nearly died out in the field. She hadn't. And she wasn't going to this time, either. Shrugging off her nerves, Abby looked around and caught the long, assessing look Hawk shot her as he pulled on a flak vest. He was sharp, she'd give him that. Clearly, he sensed her hesitation, but hell if she'd let him see her sweat. She lifted her chin and sat down.

But if she was a good actress, then he was a great

actor, because she had no idea what he was thinking behind that perpetually cynical gaze.

And she didn't care. She was here for the job. She would remain in the van, in charge of communications, while the team made their way to the farmhouse, and then to the barn a half mile beyond that, where they'd execute the raid.

"There," Watkins said to Hawk as he finished wiring him.

Hawk shrugged back into his shirt. "You fix the problem from the other day?" he asked.

Abby's eyes had wandered again to Hawk's body—bad eyes—but her ears pricked. "Problem?"

"Bad wire." Watkins lifted a shoulder. "Happens."

"It shouldn't," she said. "Make sure it doesn't."

Watkins nodded.

Hawk let his T-shirt fall over his abs, hiding the wires as his gaze again met hers. One eyebrow arched in the silent question: *Were you staring at me?*

No. No, she wasn't. To prove it, she turned to her own equipment, trying not to remember the last time she'd been wired before a raid. Elliot Gaines, the head honcho, had done her up himself.

Of course he'd had a personal interest. They'd had a burgeoning friendship, at least on her part. For his part, he clearly wished for more, far more. In any case, he couldn't have known how bad it would all go....

And it had gone extremely bad. One minute she'd been listening to Gaines's quiet, authoritative voice in her ear, telling her she was doing great, just to hold her position while his team to the west "handled it," and then the next, there'd been a 12-gauge shotgun to her temple and she'd been taken hostage.

Now, a year later, in another time and place, someone murmured something in a low voice that she couldn't quite catch, and several of the men behind her laughed softly.

Releasing tension, she knew, most likely with an off-color joke that she didn't want to hear. Living as a woman in a man's world was nothing new, but she had to admit, tonight, it was grating on her nerves.

Granted, her nerves were already scraped raw just by being here, but that was no one's fault but her own. Gaines had transferred her at her request after a leave of absence. She'd wanted to prove to herself that she could still do her job, that she hadn't let the "incident" take anything from her.

But with damp palms and butterflies bouncing in her gut, she wondered if maybe she had more to overcome than she'd thought.

"Hey."

With a start, Abby turned toward Hawk. He was geared up and ready to face the night, looking big, bad, tough and prepared for anything. She bet he didn't have any butterflies.

The others were engaged in conversation, but Hawk stood close, looking at her as if he could see her anxiety. "Ready?"

That he could see her nervousness meant she didn't have it nearly as together as she'd like. "Of course I'm ready."

"Of course," he repeated, but didn't move. "Listen, I know you're going to bite my head off for this, but I'm getting a weird vibe from you here, and—"

"I said I was fine." She swiveled back to her computer to prove it.

"All right, then." She could feel him watching her very closely. "You're fine. I'm fine. We're all fine."

She heard him turn to follow the others out the door, and glanced back to watch the long-limbed ease that didn't do a thing to hide the latent power just beneath the surface. Or the irritation.

Abby let out a rough breath. *Damn it.* He might be a hell of a charmer, but he was also a hell of an agent, and truth be told, she admired his work ethic even more than she secretly admired his body. And she wanted him to be able to admire *her* work ethic. "Hawk."

He looked back, his broad shoulders blocking the night from view, but not the chill that danced in on an icy wind. "Yeah?"

"Watch yourself."

A hint of a self-deprecating smile crossed his lips. "Thought you were doing that for me."

She felt the heat rise to her face, but he'd caught her fair and square. His smile came slow and sure, and far too sexy for her comfort.

As he left, she let out a slow breath and fanned her face.

"DAMN, IT'S BUTT-ASS COLD out here."

At Logan's statement of the obvious, Hawk blew out a breath, which changed into a puff of fog before being whipped away by the cutting wind. The two of them lay on their bellies on the battered roof of the barn that had been pinpointed as a bomb-processing plant.

And yeah, it was butt-ass cold up here, but he was more focused on the fact that he was thirty feet above the ground without a safety rope, with the wind threatening to take him to the land of Oz.

Christ, he really hated heights.

Logan lowered his binoculars to blow on his hands. "Maybe we could do this thing before we freeze to the roof like a pair of Popsicles."

Like Hawk, Logan was built with the capacity to do whatever, whenever. Tough as nails. Physically honed. Trained to be a weapon all on his own, with or without the aid of bullets. But he enjoyed complaining. Always had, and Hawk should know— they'd been together since they'd been eighteen and in boot camp. They'd gone from bunkmates to brothers and knew each other like no one else.

To get here, they'd drugged a pack of rottweilers, disabled the alarm on the farmhouse and stealthily made their way through the woods to the barn. The place was a nice setup for criminal activity. Surrounded by the sharp, jagged peaks of the Bighorn Mountains, there were also rolling hills and a maze of lakes and streams, all of which were nothing but an inky black silhouette in the dark night. No neighboring ranches, no neighboring anything except maybe bears and bison and coyotes.

And the many cars and trucks parked behind the farmhouse.

Odd. It would seem that there was a large group of people here somewhere, and yet there hadn't been a soul in the house or in any of the small storage sheds behind it.

Which left the huge barn.

An icy gust hit Hawk in the face, burning his skin. He had to admit, things had definitely gone from interesting to tricky, because now the metal tiles beneath them were icing over. Any movement could be detrimental to their health, because slipping off here meant a thirty-foot fall to the frozen earth below.

Thanks to his goggles, Hawk had a crystal-clear view of the ground, and the distance to it made him want to puke. They'd been in far worse circumstances, he reminded himself, where his fear of heights had been the least of his worries. He and Logan had done some pretty ugly shit involving some pretty ugly people. On more than one occasion, they'd managed to stay alive on instinct alone, in parts of the world that didn't even warrant being on the map.

So all in all, things had improved.

"Hope it doesn't rain, because this baby'll turn right into a giant metal slide." Logan said this calmly, because he, damn him, did not have a height issue. "Like the one at the carnival—"

"Logan?"

"Yeah?"

"Shut up."

He laughed softly.

The temperature had indeed dropped to two degrees above freezing their balls off, and with that wind icing up their organs, Hawk wanted to get a move on. But they were stuck up here until they got the signal from communications, which happened to be Abby and crew parked in a van on the main road half a mile south of here. "We need to move closer," he said to her via his mic, over a noisy gust that whipped dust from the roof and into his face.

"Remain in position," she ordered, her voice breaking with static, but still sounding soft, warm… and sexy as hell.

At least in Hawk's opinion.

Just listening to her made him react like Pavlov's dog. Only he wasn't drooling. Nope, listening to her elicited visions of wild up-against-the-wall sex, which caused a much more base reaction than slobber. "Remaining in position isn't going to work," he told her.

"Soon as I hear from Watkins and Thomas," she said, the static increasing, "we'll move."

We. As in not her. He knew she used to be a great field agent, and yeah, so he'd read her files. But all her cases had ended abruptly a year ago, and no amount of digging could produce a reason. Then, after a six-month leave, she'd transferred from Seattle to Cheyenne, where Hawk had done his best to ignore his inexplicable attraction to her, because that had seemed to work for her.

But now he wondered, how was it she'd gotten so comfortable behind the safety net? Why had she given up being in the trenches with the rest of them for a computer screen?

"Watkins and Thomas are making their way to the east and west doors beneath you," she added, referring to Logan's and Hawk's counterparts on the ground. "Wait for my cue."

Uh-huh. Easy for her to say. She sat out of the slicing wind in that van, and Hawk would bet money she had the motor running and the heater on full blast.

She'd changed on the plane, out of her skirt, the one that had messed with his mind every time it clung to her thighs, which was only with every single movement she made. But her cargo pants and long-sleeved ATF button-down clung to her, too. Hell, she could wear a potato sack and do something to him.

Logan shifted. Probably trying not to freeze to the roof. Hawk did the same, but for different reasons entirely.

"Nearly there," Thomas said into their earpieces. "Hearing noises from inside, a steady pinging."

"Affirmative," Watkins said. "The windows are blacked out, going in southwest door— *Jesus*. It's full of ammo and workstations. Definitely bomb-making going on here, guys, but there's no one in sight." He let out a low whistle. "Seriously, there's enough blow in here to make Las Vegas prime beach-front property."

"Suspects?" Abby asked.

"None."

"That can't be," she murmured.

Hawk had to agree with her. Something was off, and not just because they'd managed to get onto the premises and up here, past the alarm and a pack of hungry rottweilers without being detected. But now they'd found the proof, right beneath their noses? It was all too easy. He flicked off his mic and looked at Logan.

"You thinking what I'm thinking?" Logan asked.

"That we're being set up, instead of the other way around?"

"Bingo."

"I'm guessing we got too close, and he's unhappy with us?"

"Let's make him really unhappy and catch the SOB red-handed."

"Watkins, search the interior," Abby directed, the static now nearly overriding her voice. "Hawk, Logan, guard the exits from above."

"But where is everyone?" This from Thomas. "It's like a ghost town in here."

"There's got to be a building we haven't cased yet. Or a basement. Something," she insisted. "Find it. Find them."

"There's nothing," Watkins said from inside. "No one."

Logan cocked his head just as Hawk felt it, a slight vibration beneath them. It was hard to discern between the howling wind screeching in his ear and the sharp static on the radio, but he'd bet that they were no longer alone up here.

"What's going on?" Abby asked.

Neither Logan or Hawk answered, not wanting to give away their position in the icy darkness, which was so complete that without the night vision goggles, they couldn't have seen a hand in front of their faces. Unfortunately, the goggles couldn't cut through the heavy dust kicked up by the wind as they silently moved toward the ladder they'd commandeered and left on the northeast side.

Which was now missing. *Shit.*

"Problem," Logan said.

"What?" Abby repeated in that voice that could give a dead guy a wet dream. Hopefully Hawk wasn't going to get dead, but without the ladder there was no way down without taking a flying leap. Just the thought made him break out into a cold, slippery sweat.

Logan jerked his head to the left, and Hawk nodded. Logan would go left, and he'd go right.

"Logan," Abby said tightly. "Hawk. Check in."

"We've got company," Logan said, so calmly he sounded comatose. "We're separating to locate."

"Details," she demanded.

"Someone took our ladder."

There was silence for one disbelieving beat. "Watkins, Thomas," she snapped. "Back them up. Now."

She was sounding a little more drill sergeant and a little less sex kitten, thought Hawk. Which was good, except he must be one sick puppy because the sound of her kicking ass turned him on as much as when she'd sounded like she was kissing it.

"West side is clear," Logan reported via radio, right on cue.

"Hawk?" This from Abby. "Check in."

"Oh, I'm fine, thanks." He eyed the slippery roof,

the distance to the ground, and gave a shudder. At Abby's growl of frustration, he let slip a grim smile as he looked left, right, behind him. Another gust blew through, wailing, railing, raising both holy hell and a thick cloud of dust as the icy air sliced right through him. He couldn't see anything, any sign of Logan behind him, or anyone else.

Which could be good.

Or very, very bad.

"Where are you?" Abby asked.

In hell. Of that, Hawk had no doubt. "Logan?"

"Hawk, get down now," Logan suddenly said, and then came a click, as if he'd been cut off.

"Logan?" Hawk tapped the earpiece. Nothing. The radio was dead, but he'd get off the roof because Logan's instincts were as good as his own. He couldn't see much, but he knew there was a tall oak nearby, with branches close enough to reach and subsequently shimmy down. *All* the way down. *Christ.*

A sound came from three o'clock, and Hawk whipped his head around. Logan or enemy? Going down.

To do so, he had to shove his night vision goggles to the top of his head so that he couldn't see the ground rushing up to meet him, not that *that* helped much because he had a helluva imagination, and could picture it just fine.

The wind doubled its efforts to loosen his hold, blinding him with debris. All he could do was hold on and pray for mercy as he lowered himself, even though praying had never really worked for him.

When his feet finally touched ground, he inhaled a deep breath and nearly kissed the damn tree trunk. Instead, he drew his gun and backed to the wall of the barn. Just to his left was a window, boarded and taped, and yet he'd swear he saw a quick flash of light from within.

Someone was definitely inside.

Watkins?

Or his very secretive bomb maker?

The radio was still eerily silent, and foreboding crept up through his veins as he slipped the night-vision goggles back over his eyes and turned the corner of the barn. There his gaze landed on a door low to the ground—a cellar entrance. Before he could try the radio again, the door flipped open, catching the wind and hitting the barn wall like a bullet.

A man crawled out, silhouetted by stacks of ammo behind him, and piles of guns, *rifles*, awfully similar to the ones that had been stolen from beneath his nose. Apparently the Kiddie Bombers liked to be armed. With ATF-confiscated weapons. Hawk steadied his gun and waited for the rogue agent to reveal himself.

The man's head lifted and all Hawk's suspicions were immediately confirmed. *Gaines.*

He managed to get a shot off, then a white-hot blast knocked him flat on his ass.

2

THE BASTARD HAD shot him, point blank, and given that it felt like his lungs had collapsed, he assumed he'd taken the hit in his chest. God bless the bullet-proof vest. Stunned, gasping for air, he tried to remain conscious, but his vision had already faded on the edges and was closing in as he lay on his back, staring up at the night sky as a whole new kind of hurt made itself at home in every corner of his body....

"Hawk? Check in," Abby said in his ear.

Check in? He felt like he was checking out.... But the radio was back, good to know, and man, did she sound hot. Too bad he was floating...floating on agony, thank you very much, and utterly unable to move.

Or speak.

"Hawk."

Ah, wasn't that sweet? She sounded worried. He was touched, or would have been if he could get past the searing pain. He needed to get up, to protect himself—

A foot planted itself on his throat, and then the fire in his body sizzled along with his vision as his air supply was abruptly cut off.

By Gaines. Regional director.

Traitor.

Hawk tried to lift one of his arms to grasp at the foot on his windpipe.

"Don't bother." Gaines pressed harder. "You'll be dead soon, anyway. I just wanted you to suffer a little first, you know, for screwing with me for so long."

Hawk found himself shockingly helpless, an absolutely new and unenjoyable experience. He simply couldn't draw air, and good Christ but he felt like his chest was burning.

"Hurts like a mother, doesn't it?"

What hurt the most was that he couldn't remember if he'd managed to spit out Gaines's name before he'd gone down. In case this all went to shit, he wanted Logan to know they'd been right. That is, if the radio was even back up. "Logan—"

"Sorry. It's going to be a tragic evening all around. You're both going to die trying to double-cross the agency."

Through a haze of agony as he choked on his very last breath, he realized he was still gripping his gun. Now if only he could get the muscles in his arm to raise it. As he struggled, he heard everyone checking in.

Watkins.

Thomas.

Logan. Thank God, Logan.

Any second now they'd realize Hawk hadn't checked in as well.

That he couldn't…

"HAWK? COME IN, HAWK." Abby said this with what she felt was admirable calm, even as a bead of sweat ran between her breasts. Something was wrong, and it wasn't just that their equipment had failed—even the backup equipment—for five long minutes.

"I don't see him," Thomas radioed.

"Me either." This from Watkins.

"I'm going back up to the roof," Logan responded. "Maybe he never got down."

She expected Hawk to jump in here with laughter in his voice to say that everything was good. But he didn't. Oh, God. She needed to sit down. For several months. Because he would not joke, not at a time like this. He might be surprisingly laid-back and easy-going considering the constant, nonstop danger the job put him in, but he knew protocol. He'd been a soldier, Special Forces. He lived by the rules, and to her knowledge, always followed them. *"Hawk."*

When he still didn't answer, she visualized him. Her therapist had taught her that picturing the cause of her grievance helped.

Of course her therapist had meant the men who'd taken her hostage, but the idea behind it was the same. Hoping it would work, she concentrated on the image of Conner Hawk.

It took embarrassingly little time—like one-point-two seconds. He came to her shirtless, which she didn't—shouldn't—speculate about. The only time she'd ever seen him that way had been six months ago, on her first day. He and Logan had spent hours lying beneath a truck in the broiling hot sun, surveying a house. After the arrests, Hawk had come into the office for a change of clothing he kept in his locker.

Abby had been sitting at a table in the employee room eating lunch, her fork raised halfway to her mouth, her salad forgotten as he'd stalked past, eyes tired, several days worth of growth on his lean jaw, sunglasses shoved up to the top of his head. He'd ripped off his sweaty shirt and stood there in nothing but jeans riding dangerously low on his hips as he and Logan laughed about something while he fought with his locker door.

Ever since the hostage situation, her therapist had been promising her that her physical desire for men would eventually return, probably when she least expected it. She'd traveled a bit, visited her parents and sister in Florida, where they'd busily set her up on all the blind dates she'd allow, and yet nothing had really taken. But sitting there in that room, it had not only returned, it came back with bells and whistles.

Holy smokes.

Conner Hawk had it going on.

Unable to help herself, she'd continued to stare at him, soaking in his tanned, sinewy chest, the tattoo, the various scars that spoke of how many years he'd been doing the hero thing. His jeans had a hole in one knee and another on the opposite thigh, exposing more lean flesh.

Then he'd glanced over and caught her staring.

Unnerved, she'd dropped her fork in her lap. Unfortunately it had still been loaded with the bite she'd never taken. Ranch dressing on silk. Nicely done.

Those melting chocolate eyes had met hers, filled with that cynical amusement he was so good at. He hadn't said a word as he'd yanked a fresh, clean shirt over his head, the muscles in his biceps and quads flexing, his ridged abdomen rippling as he'd pulled the material down. His eyes, even heavy-lidded from exhaustion, had still managed to convey a heat that had exhilarated her in a way she hadn't wanted to think about.

After that, he'd never quite accepted her icy silence for what it was—a desperate cry for him to stay away, because she needed her distance.

Oh, boy, had she needed her distance. And she couldn't blame him for not really buying it. Hell, she'd definitely, at least for that one moment, given him the wrong impression. She'd given *herself* the wrong impression, because she'd wanted him— wanted his arms to come around her, wanted him to dip his head and kiss her, long and deep and wet as he slid his hands over her body, giving it the pleasure she'd denied herself all year.

But she'd come to her senses and hadn't let herself lapse again.

At least not publicly.

As the newcomer to the division, she'd made a big effort to fit in, to get to know all her co-workers, while definitely staying clear of Hawk. She'd been aloof and stand-offish with him and him alone be- cause she'd thought it best for her to keep far away until she was ready for the feelings he evoked. Which she still wasn't.

That didn't mean she didn't care, because she did. Too much. Therein lay her problem.

From that salad-in-the-lap moment, Abby had taken one look at him, past the bad boy physique, past the knowing grin, and had known.

She could care too much for this man.

Now she sat in the van, with the night whipping around them, desperately visualizing Hawk checking in because she had to believe he was okay.

Please be okay.

"Someone's down," came Watkins's voice. "Repeat, *agent down*."

Oh, God. Once upon a time, *she'd* been the agent down, and just the words brought back the stark terror.

Dark room.

Chained to a wall.

Cold, then hot, then fear like nothing she'd ever known when she'd realized her captors wanted information she didn't have, and that they were going to torture her anyway....

But this wasn't then. And what had happened to her wasn't happening now. *Concentrate*, damn it. *Focus.* "Where is he?"

The men behind her, Ken and Wayne, already in high alert from the equipment failure, worked more frantically, trying to get feed on him.

"Watkins," she said. "Clarify."

Nothing.

"Thomas, are you with Watkins?"

More of that horrifying nothing. Whipping around, she looked at the two men in disbelief. "Are we down again?"

Wayne's fingers tapped across his keyboard. "Fuck. Yes."

Was it possible for a heart to completely stop and yet pound at the same time? "They need backup." She stood to yank off her blazer.

"What are you doing?" Ken demanded.

"Getting ready." Abby tossed her useless headset aside.

"No. We're not supposed to—"

"We have at least one man down and no radio." She slapped a vest over her shirt, and then grabbed a gun, emotion sitting heavy in her voice. No cool, calm and collected now. No, all that had gone right out the window with her last ounce of common sense, apparently. "We're going in."

There was some scrambling, whether to join her or stop her she didn't know because she didn't look back as she opened the door to the van.

LOGAN BOLTED ACROSS THE ROOF of the barn, dodging the icy spots and the shadow he'd seen. Not Gaines, but one of his paid goons, coming back from where he'd last spotted Hawk.

He sped up, high-tailing his way toward Hawk, because that's what they did, they backed each other up. They'd been doing so for years in far tighter jams than this one. And in all that time, he'd never once felt anything but utterly invincible.

But at this moment, all he felt was terror.

Hawk was down.

Rounding a corner of the roof, Logan headed toward a vent. As he crouched down behind it to survey the situation, the air stirred, and he felt a blinding pain in the back of his neck. As he whipped around to fight, he was hit again, by a two-by-four, or so it felt, and then he was flying off the roof toward the ground.

Shit. Now both he and Hawk were down....

THIS WAS RIDICULOUS, ABBY TOLD herself as the cold, icy night slapped her face. She'd taken herself *out* of the field. She'd vowed that nothing could get her back to it. And yet here she was, off and running at the first sign of trouble because she couldn't stand the thought of an agent down.

Ken caught up with her, both of them gasping in the shockingly bitter wind. They took the long, winding dirt path up toward the ranch. The place sat on a set of rolling hills that looked deceptively mild and beautiful by day. But by night the area turned almost sinister, steep, rugged and dangerously isolated. Fallen pine needles crunched beneath their feet. The patches of ice were lethal spots of menace that could send them flying, but still they ran.

The wind didn't help. It was picking up, if that was possible, slicing through to the very bone, kicking up a dusty haze that nothing could cut through, not even the night vision goggles.

When they reached the dark farmhouse, they stopped to draw air into their burning lungs.

"Around the back," Ken said. "The barn's around the back."

She was already moving that way but came to a stop at the corner of the farmhouse, where she had the vantage point of what should have been a woodsy clearing, but with the dark and the driving winds, seemed more like the wilds of Siberia.

She knew the barn lay beyond the trees, but in between there were no lights, no sign of human life. Abby went left, Ken right, both skirting the edges of the clearing, using the trees as cover.

Where was everyone?

As she came through the woods, the barn loomed up ahead, nothing but a black outline against a black sky. And then she saw him.

Hawk.

He was standing, holding his gun pointed at someone standing in the door of the barn.

Abby watched in horror as the gun flashed, and she caught a glimpse of the man he'd aimed at flying backward like a rag doll.

Gaines? Elliot Gaines? What the hell? Why was he here? Everything within her went cold. Had Hawk just shot Gaines?

3

WINNING WAS EVERYTHING. Knowing it, Gaines pushed down harder on Hawk's windpipe, barely feeling the blood running down his arm. He'd been nicked before, a year and a half ago in Seattle as a matter of fact, while wrestling in the dark with one of his own ATF agents.

Hawk, in fact.

See, that's what happened when one hired the best, and Hawk was the best of the best. He was a fucking pitbull, and he'd all but publicly promised to stop at nothing until the leader of the Kiddie Bombers was behind bars.

He might as well have signed his own death certificate.

And goddamn, he'd actually gotten a shot off. That was a pisser. But the explosions Gaines's men had rigged would go off soon, and Hawk would be lost in them. Logan also, because it had become clear tonight that there was no other way.

And though it killed him, Abby, too.

No loose ends.

And there wouldn't be. Thanks to his crew, which

included Watkins working on the inside, everything had been perfectly choreographed. Already Tibbs would have received an anonymous tip that would raise enough questions about Hawk's "role" in the theft of the rifles from the ATF to enable Tibbs to get a search warrant for Hawk's place. There he'd find a computer memory stick with Kiddie Bombers' information, including purchases, sales and contacts, password-protected and encrypted just enough to make it look legit.

Hawk framed, check. Hawk dead, almost check.

And then, retirement time. Good times. The only thing that would have made tonight perfect would have been if he hadn't been forced to take out Abby. He regretted that, and he'd miss her like hell, but he couldn't risk the rest of his life for a piece of tail, no matter how badly he wanted that piece.

He was so close now. Close enough to taste it. God, he loved to win. And tonight, he planned to win big. "Got any last-minute prayers?"

EVEN WITH HIS VEST, the after-effects of taking a slug in the chest were brutal. His muscles were spasming, his body twitching, and it was sheer agony to get his limbs to obey his mind. But Hawk managed to grab Gaines's ankle and yank him to the ground, leveling the playing field, though not by much. Jesus, even his brain hurt, feeling as if it'd been used as a pinball within his skull. Gathering his thoughts was an exercise in futility, but he had to fight off Gaines—then he caught the flicker from

within the barn. Flames. Ah, shit, the whole thing
was going to—

Blow.

The explosion knocked them both backward. The
barn roof blew sky high, catching the grass in the
clearing on fire, as well as the trees.

Surrounded. He was surrounded by unrelenting
heat, scorching him both inside and out. Gaines came
up on his knees, looking like death warmed over as
he staggered to his feet, pointing his gun. "You're
hard to kill."

"So are you." Hawk's gaze locked on the dark spot
blooming out from the shoulder of Gaines's jacket.
"Missed your black heart, unfortunately. I blame the
hit to the chest. Threw me off."

The smoke rose from behind Gaines's head,
making it look like steam was coming out of his ears.

"It's going to get worse," his own personal monster said.

It was true. If Gaines chose to shoot Hawk in the
nuts, there was nothing he could do. His body was
shit at the moment.

Gaines pointed the gun between Hawk's eyes.

"Go to hell," Hawk said.

Gaines grinned. "Tell you what, I'll meet you there."

Hawk's life flashed before his eyes. His parents,
gone now, but so proud of him when they'd been
alive. Special Forces, where he'd had a good run—
no, make that a great run—before moving to ATF.

Another great run.

Until now.

Maybe he should have added some more personal touches to his life's canvas. A wife. Kids. But he'd always figured there was plenty of time for that.

Helluva time to be wrong. "Do it," he said, coughing from the smoke. "And die."

Gaines laughed. "You have no idea how right you are. Now give me your gun."

Hawk tossed it over, then attempted to keep breathing. Not easy when his chest was still on fire, and actual flames were leaping all around them. He had no idea why he was alive but just in case it didn't last, he kicked his foot out and again swiped Gaines's legs from beneath him. They rolled, and he got two strong punches into his superior's gut before he lost the element of surprise and Gaines clocked him in the jaw, and then his ribs.

Unlike Tibbs, Gaines had no soft middle. He was built like a boxer, one who trained 24/7. On a good day, he'd be a tough opponent in a fight, but tonight, with Hawk in agony, was not a good day. They fought dirty and hard, and the bitch of it was, Hawk had no idea what the hell had happened—why had Gaines come after him? He fisted his hands in Gaines's shirt, and the material ripped, revealing…

A puckered scar over his collar bone. From a bullet. Goddamn, his proof had just literally appeared. "I did hit you that night," he breathed. "I did. I fucking hit you."

"But I lived." Panting heavily, Gaines grinned. "Guess you need more target practice, huh?"

The heat from the blast and the flames licking at

them had sweat streaming into Hawk's eyes. He couldn't see anything but Gaines's face and a wall of flames.

They had to finish this thing off now, one way or another, or they were both going to die. Hawk swiped more sweat from his eyes and gasped to draw air into his taxed lungs. "So running the whole division wasn't good enough for you, you had to put illegal weapons back on the street? Why didn't you just kill a bunch of innocent people yourself?"

Gaines's jaw tightened. He was holding onto his shoulder with his free hand, assuring Hawk that he'd been hurt more than he wanted to show. "I'm going to kill you instead."

"I'm not dying tonight."

"We're both dying tonight. Only difference is that my death's going to be fake. Well, that and the fact that you're going out as the bad guy."

"You're insane. No one will ever believe that."

"Abby will."

Abby. *Abby?* What the hell did she have to do with this?

"She's out there, you know." Gaines jerked his chin in the direction of the clearing.

Hawk was just stunned enough to crane his head and look, but all he saw were those flickering flames coming ever closer, so close he could feel the hairs on his arm singing. "What are you talking about? She's in the van." Safe and sound.

God, please let her be in the van, safe and sound.

Gaines shrugged. "Let's just say the hero worship

I've built up with her is going to finally pay off for me, however briefly. Along with the news that Tibbs has just discovered evidence that you've been running the Kiddie Bombers." He *tsked*. "Shame on you."

Hawk had no idea what the hell Gaines was talking about. He couldn't see Abby. Hell, he couldn't see anything beyond the smoke, but Abby wouldn't leave the van.

And yet he remembered how she'd lost her 1-900 voice when she'd sounded worried about him.

Or so he'd assumed…

He hadn't survived all he'd survived without seeing the ugly side of human nature. Maybe she hadn't been worried for him at all, but for Gaines. Ah, God, the thought of her in cahoots with the bad guy put a sharp pain right through him. A new pain, over and above the others, and that was saying something.

"Once Abby realizes I'm here and that I'm missing, she'll want to save me," Gaines mocked. "Too little, too late, of course."

Hawk willed his damn muscles to obey the commands his brain was sending. Get up. *Kick his ass.* "Abby's done with you. She turned you in," he improvised.

Gaines went utterly still. "Bullshit."

"Are you willing to gamble on it?" he taunted, biding time, trying to figure a way out of this mess.

Gaines straightened to scan the horizon, still holding his shoulder as he searched for someone.

Abby?

"If that's true, I'll have to up my timeline."

Oh, Christ. "You won't find her." Because Hawk would get to her first. He began to inch backward. He had no idea where he thought he could escape to, but it was time to go. He'd managed to get a foot away when another explosion rang out, raining down fiery fragments on top of them. The smoke was so thick Hawk couldn't breathe, couldn't see, but he sure as hell could keep moving, and he hightailed it as fast as he could.

"Goddamn you!" came Gaines's howl of fury at Hawk's escape.

Using the choking smoke as a screen, Hawk dodged into the woods, past the flames and grabbed a tree for support. Christ, he felt as if he'd been run over by a Mack truck.

Sinking all the way to the spinning ground seemed like a good idea. He did manage to roll to his back, where he studied the smoke-filled sky. Though he couldn't see anything without his night goggles, which had slid off, oh, somewhere about the time that Gaines had given him a nice one-two punch to the left kidney, he could hear sirens. Fire engines, probably cops, too. Lots of them.

Because somehow Gaines had managed to frame him for everything *he'd* done, which was plenty.

God, he was so screwed.

ABBY COULDN'T BREATHE. Yes, she'd just run a half mile in less than two minutes, and was now inhaling only smoke as she stared in horror at the barn, engulfed in flames, but that wasn't why she couldn't catch any air in her lungs.

Had she really seen Hawk shoot Gaines before the explosion? She'd left the van in such a hurry that she hadn't taken a radio. The only personal effects she carried were her gun, cell phone and the mini credit card she had attached to it in case of emergencies. She'd already called Tibbs. He'd told her that according to Thomas, Logan had fallen from the roof and was waiting for a helicopter to airlift him to Cheyenne Memorial Hospital. No word from Hawk.

God. The whole night had blown up in their faces. She'd asked Tibbs about Gaines being here, and he said he'd check and get back to her. In the meantime, gun drawn, she tried to get closer to the barn but the heat stopped her. She couldn't see a thing, and she couldn't get closer.

And then her cell vibrated. "Gaines *is* there," Tibbs drawled. "Apparently, he came to watch the takedown."

"Oh, my God." So if she hadn't imagined Gaines, then she probably hadn't imagined Hawk shooting him either. Still holding her phone to her ear, she took off again but immediately tripped, falling flat on her face and losing her grip on her gun. Twisting around to see what she'd fallen over, she saw a roof shingle, and…a rifle?

"Abigail?"

"I'm here, Tibbs. I'm okay." Crawling to the rifle, she picked it up, burning her fingers. She dropped it, but she didn't need to access her computer to guess that the serial number on this rifle would match one of the ones stolen from their storage.

Was that why Gaines had come—had he suspected the Kiddie Bombers had taken the illegal weapons for their own personal use?

And why had Hawk shot him?

"Gaines radioed his office that he'd gotten into the barn," Tibbs told her.

"The barn is on fire."

"Did he get out?"

"On it." After spending a few futile minutes trying to find her gun, she checked the rifle. Loaded. She slipped the leather strap over her shoulder and took a deep breath for courage. You can still do this. All around her the flames leaped and crackled and burned brighter, spurred on by the vicious wind.

Knowing she had to hurry, she moved deeper into the woods to get around the fire, staggering to a halt at the unholy howling of a wolf that sounded far too close. Could be worse, she told herself. Could be a grizzly.

Some branches rustled and she nearly swallowed her tongue as she rushed into motion, her shoes crunching on the frozen ground as she circled back in toward the barn, determined to get to the bottom of this crazy evening.

She passed no one, and not for the first time felt unnerved by that fact. How was the place so utterly deserted? None of it made any sense.

Unless.

Oh, God. Unless it had been a setup from the start. At the realization, her feet faltered, and she slipped on the rocky terrain but caught herself in time on a tree only twenty feet from the barn. Abby wanted so badly to wake up, to know that she wasn't losing her mind.

She thought she knew Hawk, and sometimes she'd even felt as if he knew her, which was exceptionally crazy because she'd never let him in at all. But, God, the thought of him being a bad guy was like a knife to the gut.

Again her cell phone vibrated. She flipped it open.

"Where are you?" Watkins demanded.

"I'm—"

"I know, I've handled it," he said.

Abby went absolutely still. "What?"

"Nothing, talking into my radio."

Wait—radio? He was talking into his radio? But the radios were down. And now her heart was in her throat. *I've handled it*…those three words brought her directly back to another raid, and another extremely bad time.

They'd been the words Gaines had spoken before she'd gone in that day, and then later, she'd heard those words from the men who'd held her. They'd spoken the words *handled it* into a radio to some unseen boss.

No. Had to be coincidental. Of course it was.

"Where are you?" Watkins asked tensely. "Why the hell did you leave the safety of the van? I need you to get back to the safety of the van, Abby. Do you copy?"

She opened her mouth to answer him but stopped herself.

Not saying a word was stepping over a line, a big one, but she didn't speak. Couldn't. Because who the hell was the bad guy here? Hawk?

Or…Watkins?

God, she was losing it.

"Abby?"

Yeah. That was her. But instead of responding, she quietly shut her phone and kept hugging the tree because suddenly her legs didn't want to hold her.

She'd seen Hawk shoot Gaines. Hawk, gun in his hand, shoot point-blank. That made it him.

Right?

Her brain hurt, physically hurt. She couldn't process it all, or make sense of it. Who to trust? Knowing she had only herself, she pushed away from the tree and ran—

And then tripped over…oh, God…a man sprawled on the ground, far too close to the flickering flames. "Elliot—" Dropping to her knees, Abby set her hands on his back and realized her mistake instantly.

This body was one solid muscle. With a moan, he rolled to his back, keeping his eyes closed beneath dark lashes and the straight dark lines of his eyebrows, which were furrowed together.

Hawk.

4

ABBY CROUCHED OVER HAWK and checked for a pulse, which he had. Relieved, she got to her feet and peered through the trees that were providing them cover. Out there she could see the barn. The side door was open, fire ripping outward, drawn by the cold, chilly oxygen. Beyond them, she could see…oh, God…boxes and boxes of ammo. She ran back to Hawk. *"Hawk."*

"Present."

She had no idea whose side he was on, but she sure as hell wasn't going to leave him here to die. "Get up."

"Sure." But he didn't move. And in spite of herself, everything within her softened. It was nothing personal, she tended to soften for injured animals and wayward children, too. It helped that he didn't look like his usual strong, capable self all sprawled on the ground. "That was a direct order."

"I'm hearing ya."

She put her hand on his jaw and looked at his mouth, which was usually curved in amusement, at her, at himself, at life. But at the moment, it was tight. Grim. Reflecting pain. She never thought she'd miss that smile, but she did. "Come on, get up, you cocky, smug SOB."

He lifted his head, and she found herself leveled flat by his soft brown eyes that were so in contrast to his definitively unsoft demeanor. Even flat on his back, he looked lean and angular and startlingly attractive as that mouth curved slightly. "Abby."

How, while completely surrounded by such utter chaos, she could feel an odd zing, she had no idea. But just looking at him made her feel dangerously feminine. "Where's Gaines?" she asked.

Hawk's short, almost buzzed hair was dusted with dirt and ash and stood straight up, revealing his hairline and a nasty cut, oozing blood. "In hell," he answered, voice rusty. "If there's any justice."

Oh, God. So it was true. Regret, and a huge sadness welled inside her. Once Gaines had saved her. Picked up the broken pieces and helped her put herself back together again. And she hadn't been able to return the favor. "So he's—"

"Not yet, he's not." His face hardened, his eyes so intense on hers that she'd have fallen to her knees if she hadn't already been there.

"I saw you shoot him," she said.

"Did you?" He grimaced. "Trust me—"

"Are you kidding?" Abby managed a laugh. He hadn't even tried to deny it. "After what I saw tonight, I should trust a rat's ass over you."

"Look, whatever you're thinking, you've got it wrong." His gaze shifted past her as he carefully scanned the immediate area, making her shiver at the danger sparking from his eyes. "He set this whole game up tonight."

Okay, clearly he was delusional, but she still had to get him away from the flames. "What hurts?"

His laugh was short and harsh. "Only every fucking inch."

Well, that they could deal with. "Get up."

"Any minute now, I swear." He closed his eyes. "So, a cocky, smug SOB? Really?"

"Come on, Hawk." He might be eyeing the flames licking at them with an eerie calm, but she was not. She hoped like hell Elliot had indeed gotten out. "Get up!"

He shifted to do just that. "Check our sixes."

"What?"

"Our asses, Ab. Make sure we're not being made. Gaines has a crew out here tonight, somewhere. They're setting explosions and making merry."

She added *paranoid* to the list. Which, given his situation, made sense. "I've got your damn ass, Hawk." Fine as it was. Crawling around behind him, she slid her arms beneath his, wrapping them around his chest so that she could pull him to safety.

"Ah, that's so sweet," he murmured. "But now's not a good time for me."

She grated her teeth. This. This was one reason why she'd stayed her distance. The man exuded raw sex appeal. Only problem? He knew it. "Don't flatter yourself." She tugged. "Do you have to be so big?"

Though his eyes remained closed, he flashed a smile straight out of her very secret fantasies—pure wicked, mischievous promise. "You don't know the half of it."

Okay, if she ever got him out of here, she was going to kill him herself.

"You smell pretty," he whispered.

Her gaze swiveled back to his, but his eyes were still closed.

"You always smell pretty…"

"You're dreaming," Abby said flatly.

"Nah. If I was dreaming, I wouldn't be this close to begging you to finish me off." But he tried to stand up, then inhaled sharply at the movement and promptly choked on the smoke. "Yeah. You really do smell amazing. Sexy."

Now *she* choked. "Stop it."

"Really sexy. Even when you're blasting me with your glacial stare."

"Shut up, Hawk."

"You don't glare at Logan," he said thoughtfully. "Or Watkins. Or anyone. Just me."

Well, that was just true enough to have her drawing in her own sharp breath as he staggered to his feet. "You don't like me much," he told her, rolling his shoulder as if it hurt.

"That's not true. I like you plenty when you're not talking."

He sighed. "Now, see, I think I'd like you plenty if you were naked."

"You're such an asshole."

"Asshole Hawk. Yeah, that fits—"

The next explosion was small but way too close

and very hot. Instinctively, she pushed him back, knocking them both down. Then she was enveloped in Hawk's strong arms and rolled, tucked into him while embers rained down.

When it was over, she realized that the muscles in his arms were quaking. He was a dead weight on top of her. "Hawk?"

A litany of swear words escaped him, blowing her hair back. He lifted his head, his eyes not even close to warm and soft, but hard as aged whiskey. "Don't ever do that again."

"What? Save your sorry ass?"

"Exactly. Save your own first, you hear me?"

"Then get moving!"

"Yeah." With a groan, he got to his feet and reached out a hand to help her. A considerate bad guy.

Where was Gaines…?

Having been in a bad situation before, the worst, Abby had a gut-wrenching need for everyone to be okay and accounted for, even knowing that someone on her team had caused all this. "Do you think Gaines—"

"Oh, that's right. You still need to rescue your Sugar Daddy."

No one at ATF knew that she'd dated him twice, she'd made sure of that. Their relationship mostly consisted of her miraculous rescue, and then a vague, uncomfortable friendship that she'd had difficulty maintaining because of her new "issues."

"Where is he, Hawk?" When he didn't answer,

she shook her head and turned toward the direction of the barn.

"No, wait. Don't." Hawk grabbed her arm, his eyes dark with concern. For her. And though it shouldn't have, it touched her as he spoke. "Don't even think about going back—"

"I have to."

"Goddamnit, Ab—"

Yanking free, she was halfway to the barn when her cell vibrated. Pulling it out of her pocket, she flipped it open and saw "unknown" ID. "Hello?"

"It's me."

Elliot's unmistakable voice brought a wave of relief. *"Where are you—"*

"Listen to me. We've been betrayed. By Hawk."

She processed the words, but, damn, it was hard to swallow, despite what she'd seen with her own eyes. "Elliot, are you sure, because—"

"Have I ever been wrong?"

Okay, no. No, he hadn't. And she knew exactly what she owed him, but— "Whose phone are you calling me on, because it's not yours—"

"Trust me, Abby."

She wanted to. She knew he wanted her to. But just because she hadn't ever allowed Hawk's charm to melt away her panties didn't mean she didn't know that he was an incredibly good ATF agent, one who believed in what he did and believed in putting away the bad guys. There had to be an explanation for all of this. "Tell me where you are—"

Another explosion interrupted her, picking her up

like a rag doll, tossing her once again on her ass in the dirt. *Damn.* Crawling back through the trees to where she'd left Hawk, she realized three extremely unsettling facts at once.

Gaines had disconnected.

Hawk was gone.

And she was all alone.

This night just kept getting better and better.

5

HAWK STUMBLED THROUGH the burning forest, getting his strength back as he made his way through the fiery night. Things had gone FUBAR quickly—"fucked up beyond all repair"—but he knew Gaines planned on somehow vanishing for good, and he couldn't let that happen. What he really needed right now was Logan, and he wished like hell he still had a radio.

But, really, he was lucky to still have his head.

He knew Abby was going to be pissed at the disappearing act, but he'd have to deal with that later. And if it turned out she wasn't in with Gaines, well, then he'd apologize and they'd all go back to their regularly scheduled program.

Which was her ignoring him. One of these days he'd figure out why her pissiness was such a turn-on....

Hawk made it around to the back of the barn before he fell to his hands and knees hard. Staring down at the dirt, he tried to gather his wits. Not easy, since they'd been scrambled by the explosions and then again by the knowledge that his boss had been playing both sides, selling the weapons they'd confiscated over the years on the black market, in essence undoing all the good they'd accomplished by putting those weapons right back into the hands of gangbangers, murderers and terrorists.

If he thought about it too long, it hurt his brain all the more. But it sure made sense. No matter how hard they'd worked at getting to the top of the Kiddie Bombers' hierarchy, they'd been thwarted at every turn.

But Gaines hadn't worked alone. No way. So who else was involved…Abby? And if not her, then who?

Watkins? Thomas?

Tibbs?

Not for the first time, he slapped at his pockets and his belt, but all forms of communication had been stripped from him in the fight. He'd even managed to lose his cell phone.

"We can't get in because of the explosions."

Hawk's ears perked at the male voice. Who was that? Thomas?

"On Gaines's last transmission, he said that Hawk did this, all of it."

No, not Thomas, Hawk thought as he used a tree to silently push himself to his feet and peer through the trees at the figures he could barely make out.

"Gaines is presumed dead."

Watkins. Watkins was the inside help Gaines had most likely needed.

"No," came an answering female voice. A shaken one. "We don't know that he's dead."

Abby. Sweet, hot Abby, with those gorgeous baby blues that softened whenever she smiled.

And hardened whenever she looked at Hawk.

He'd been looked at that way by women before, usually after a few drinks and an overnighter, when he'd made his excuses rather than stick around and explain that he was only saving the woman some time because he wasn't a good long-term bet.

Hell, he wasn't even a good medium-term bet.

No sweat, he'd always figured. He'd get back to the whole love game when he retired from the job.

Which wasn't looking so good right now.

Abby had pulled out her cell, and was listening. "Yes, sir." Slapping the phone shut, she let out a breath. "Tibbs found a memory stick in Hawk's house." She hesitated. "With information on the Kiddie Bombers."

Ah, Christ. He'd been set up but good. *Thanks, Gaines.*

"If Gaines is dead…" Watkins trailed off, but Hawk silently finished the sentence in his own head.

Then I go up for murder.

The men around Abby moved off, probably to search for him. Get in line, he thought.

Gaines had really gotten it together for this one. If he had his way, Hawk would die tonight. Probably Logan, too.

And…oh, Christ. If Hawk had succeeded in even planting a seed of doubt in Gaines's mind about Abby turning him in, then he'd screwed her.

Gaines would have to off her, too.

Whether she'd been in with Gaines no longer mattered, she was now a target right alongside Hawk. If something happened to her, it'd be his fault. *Shit.* Gulping in a deep breath, he pushed off from the tree and whipped around to pursue Abby.

To keep her safe.

But he only got about two steps before he plowed directly into a brick wall. A soft, perfumed brick wall.

Flying through the air, he realized the person trying to kill him had an instantly recognizable body and scent. Flowers, and some sort of sexy light spice that made him think of both sweetness and heat at the same time.

Of Abby, who'd wrapped her arms around him hard, and as they both sailed through the hazy air, heading toward the frozen earth, he had time to think one more thing.

Goddamn, but he was getting tired of eating dirt tonight.

ABBY SKIDDED ACROSS the unforgiving ground. She felt it digging into her legs, felt the damp chill her skin, but that was the least of her problems as Hawk rolled, pressing her into the ground with his body, which was taut and extremely primed for violence. Before she could so much as draw a smoke-filled breath, he clamped a hand over her mouth, completely immobilizing her, which promptly brought her back to another time and place. All her training flew out the window as terror took over, leaving her fighting like a wild thing, ineffective and serving only to drain her energy.

"Stop." Hawk's voice came low and gravelly, his mouth so close to her ear that she felt his lips brush her skin. "I'm not going to hurt you, but I can't vouch for Gaines, so save it."

The night and smoke combined to create an unwanted intimacy, as did his weight over her. They were away from the barn, in the trees, out of sight. But still, she held out hope that any second now Ken or Watkins or *someone* was going to help her. Then she'd find Elliot and get to the bottom of this crazy night.

"I'm going to take my hand away," Hawk murmured. "But we're going to stay just like this. Real quiet, okay?"

She nodded. Of course she nodded, but the minute he lifted away his fingers, she spit out *"Get off me!"*

He sighed and again covered her mouth, which made her struggle like mad beneath him. She was beyond frightened, but he was calm, breathing so normally she wanted to scream in frustration.

"Abby, goddamn it, *stop*."

She tried to bite his fingers but he just pressed harder on her mouth. The low light cast his face in soft shadows, softening his features, making him seem almost vulnerable. Which was ridiculous given that she was the vulnerable one here!

"Are you with Gaines?" he asked.

What?

He was watching her very carefully. "I need to

know. Which side are you on?" Slowly he lifted his hand from her mouth.

"I'm on the *good* side!"

Hawk stared at her. "I have no idea if you're lying—"

"I'm not!"

His jaw brushed hers as he nodded, and she became extremely aware of how he held her. Tightly. Too tightly to move. And yet somehow, incredibly gently.

What kind of a bad guy cared if he hurt her or not?

"Just had to make sure." He said this lightly, as if they were having tea and cookies instead of lying on the ground. "So if you're not a bad guy, that means you—what came back to help me?"

"Yes," she lied, closing her eyes for a moment to protect her thoughts, which were that she wished she could help him. She wished she could connect what she'd seen to what her heart was telling her—that this man, this fierce, intense, wildly sexy man couldn't have possibly done what she saw him do. She gauged his weight. "I came back to help you." Take you in. "Hawk…" She had to, Abby reminded herself, and though she had no idea what made her say it, she whispered, "I'm sorry," and then came up hard with her knee between his legs.

When he slumped over her and let out his breath in a soft *whoosh*, she played the rolling game as well as he had a moment ago and ended up on top, straddling his hips, breasts pressed to his chest, hands entwined with his on either side of his head to hold him down. Then she made the monumental mistake of looking into his face.

His eyes met hers in the dark night, reflecting the fact that despite his easy-going tone, he was in some serious pain. "Good one," he wheezed and coughed. "Holy shit."

Remorse was a luxury she couldn't afford, no matter how much she was attracted to him or how good an agent she'd thought him to be. She wouldn't make the mistake of thinking she had the upper hand for long. He'd been Special Forces, and he was considered a deadly weapon even when completely naked, so she knew the truth—if Hawk wanted to get away from her, he could. "I'm going to have to call for backup," she said slowly, watching him, overwhelmingly aware of his body tensed with barely repressed aggression beneath hers. She hadn't been this close physically to a guy in a year.

A year, two weeks and three days.

But who was counting?

Why was he letting her hold him down?

She didn't know, but she needed the rifle, and began to reach back for it—

"Don't." He tried flashing a grin. "Come on. We don't need backup. You and I can rock and roll all on our own."

"I'm not hitting on you, and you know it. I've never hit on you."

"Really."

"Really."

"So that time I caught you staring at me changing shirts, you were, what—checking for moles?"

Okay, he had her there. "I was not hitting on you," she repeated stiffly. "Good God, only an idiot would think that!"

"An ass *and* an idiot." He sounded amused. "I had no idea how highly you thought of me."

"You shot Gaines," she reminded him, watching him very carefully. She knew better than most how fast the man could move.

"So we're going to talk shop now?" he asked, as if he hadn't just held her down against her will. Maybe he'd decided she was no threat. That she wouldn't scream to get help when she needed it.

Too bad he was dead wrong.

"Because up until now you haven't been all that interested. Unless…unless it's the opposite. You've just been playing hard to get." Hawk grinned again, but it was forced.

And, yes, she actually knew the difference between his real smile and a forced one. But she'd obsess over that later. For right now, Abby wasn't going to let him distract her, not when he was as slick as rain, and she could feel him beneath her, gathering strength, his every muscle poised for action. She very carefully shifted her weight and…

He almost let her get the rifle, too. But then he locked his gaze on hers, his filled with a whole host of things she wished she couldn't see—regret, resignation and also sadness, which she didn't understand. The next thing she knew, he'd unarmed her and once again she found herself held down by six feet two inches of solid muscle.

"Where did you get the rifle?"

"I found it after the first explosion."

"Or you got it from Gaines, out of the barn. Damn it." He shifted, pressing down harder.

Her windpipe closed, her heart stopped and she thought maybe the world had slowed to a halt on its axis. Abby opened her mouth to scream, but again his hand came down over it.

"No, don't. I can't let you shoot me, or call for help," he said with real remorse in his voice as he threw the strap of the rifle over his shoulder. His eyes were black, fathomless pools, unwavering in their intensity as they fixed on her. "I'm sorry you're scared. I'm not going to hurt you."

Ha, she tried to say. *I'm not scared.* But she was so far beyond scared she couldn't even speak the lie.

Hawk sighed and leaned in a little closer. She could feel his chest pressing into her breasts, the powerful thigh he'd shoved between hers. He still had one hand on her mouth, the other gripping her wrists high above her head. He wasn't hurting her, though he outweighed her by a good seventy pounds. "Any more weapons I need to know about?" he asked, shifting slightly and releasing the hand on her wrists in order to frisk her. As he did, her nose brushed against his neck. His hand slid down her body intimately, choking a gasp out of her. His scent was a surprisingly good one given the night he'd had.

"No screaming," he reminded her. "Promise me."

She nodded her head. She'd have promised him the moon if he'd only get the hell off her so that she could draw air into her aching lungs. Besides, she was banking on someone, anyone, discovering them any second now.

He nodded in return. "Good. Because I'm having a major guilt attack here, and I really just need you to cooperate." That said, he lifted his fingers from her mouth.

Immediately, she opened her mouth to yell, but he stopped her but good.

This time with his mouth.

She was so stunned, it actually took Abby a moment to struggle. He was kissing her.

Really.

Kissing.

Her.

And, holy smokes, she had to work frantically to actually keep herself distanced…which turned out to be all but impossible with his lips slanting over hers, his tongue licking the inside of her mouth, consuming her, heating her up from the inside.

God. Six months of wondering how it'd feel to have his hands on her hadn't come close to the reality, but this wasn't the time to melt. No. No melting. This went against every thing she'd expected, against everything she'd experienced the last time a man held her down, and she didn't know how to react.

But Hawk did. Oblivious to her inner torment, he

kept on kissing her. And if she'd thought accidentally brushing her nose against his neck had been heart attack inducing, it was nothing compared to mouth on mouth. His lips were surprisingly soft and yet somehow firm, and while she processed that realization, another came right on its heels.

She'd frozen like a scared little bunny, when she'd promised herself no more scared little bunny. It was why she'd talked Gaines into letting her come back to work after the leave of absence, it was why she'd chosen communications, where she could be in the action and yet not in danger.

Ha!

His tongue traced her lower lip, then slipped inside her mouth to tango with hers, reminding her she was in danger now, mortal danger of forgetting where they were.

Oh, no. Nope. Not happening. Again she came up hard with her knee.

But she'd lost the element of surprise, and he anticipated the move, shifting so that she caught him in the upper thigh instead as he kept kissing her.

She'd shoot him. Soon as she got her rifle back, that is. He still had one of his powerful legs between hers, pressed up high enough that she couldn't swallow without him feeling it, but she squirmed anyway. He merely pressed down harder, and unbelievably, it awakened parts of her that had been dormant for a long time.

Then he lifted his head, his breathing none too steady as he stared at her. "Two things. Gaines wants me dead, and I think he wants you the same. I need you to believe me."

"No—"

"Goddamnit—" Hawk bit back the curse, then shook his head. "Fine. You won't trust me, then I have no choice."

Reaching back, he grabbed something from his pocket. Handcuffs.

Abby met his gaze and at what she saw there, felt like she was straddling a steep crevice, about to plunge to a helluva fall. "Hawk."

"Sorry."

"Whoa. Wait a damn minute—"

He slapped the steel on one of her wrists and then on one of his, linking them together.

6

WATKINS STOOD ON THE EDGE of the clearing, feeling the heat of the fire toast his face. The wind lashed at him, the smoke stinging his eyes. He'd directed Gaines's men out of there now that the explosions had gone off, and the fire was out of control.

Their job was done. Permanently. Most would vanish completely now with the booty Gaines had given each of them, although it was inevitable that some, the greedy ones, would continue with their illegal forays.

Not his problem.

His cell vibrated. He looked down at the readout and grimaced. He debated not answering, but that could be bad for his health. "Yeah?"

"How the hell did Logan get onto a heli-transport?" Gaines demanded. "He's supposed to be dead. You were supposed to have him killed."

Watkins closed his eyes. He'd been paid extremely well over the years, and, as a result, he hadn't had a problem with how tonight was to go down.

But he hadn't agreed to off Logan.

Nor Abby.

Besides, there wasn't enough money to look into Abby's eyes and watch her die. There just wasn't. "Not my fault. Sam screwed up and didn't make sure he was dead before he tossed him off the roof. And then Abby ordered me to—"

"Christ. You let a woman run your show? You're worthless."

The back of Watkins's neck tingled. His heart lodged in his throat. He turned in a slow circle, making it halfway around before he came face-to-face with two hooded men.

Gaines's men. "I thought I told you guys to get out of here."

"Goodbye, Watkins," Gaines said in his ear, just as one of the men lifted his gun and pointed it at Watkins's chest.

J.T. LOGAN WAS DREAMING ABOUT floating on a raft, surrounded by a sea of gorgeous, stacked *Playboy* centerfolds there to serve his every whim. Even dead asleep he knew the utter ridiculousness of the fantasy, and exactly how politically incorrect it was, but, hey, it wasn't his fault, he was dreaming.

But it didn't last long enough. As he came awake in slow degrees, pain spread like knives stabbing throughout his entire body.

Holy shit. With a moan, he opened his eyes and found himself staring up at one of his *Playboy* centerfolds. *Huh?* Still dreaming? Hard to tell. She wasn't picture-perfect like the others nor magazine-

cover ready, but there was something vibrant, something extremely real about her.

She wore blue, which contrasted with her siren-
red hair, pulled into two haphazard braids on either
side of her head. She was watching over him from
behind black-rimmed glasses through which a pair
of forest-green eyes, outlined by long, spiky lashes,
blinked at him. These rather amazing eyes were
narrowed, and her forehead was creased into a frown,
with one eyebrow bisected by a scar that drew his
gaze.

He couldn't look away. Oddly, he wanted to know
what had happened to cause that scar more than he
wanted to know why his head felt as if it'd been
blown half off his shoulders.

She wore no makeup except for gloss on lips that
were still frowning and also moving.

Asking him a question, he realized. Unfortunately, he couldn't seem to hear a thing.

Yeah, he had to still be dreaming. But what was
this harassed-looking, slightly rumpled *Playboy*
bunny doing in his dreams?

The others had all been naked, and yet here she
sat wearing clothes. Scrubs to be exact, which wasn't
one of his particular fantasies, though he was always
willing to—

Uh-oh.

Turning his head, he took in the sky. Ah. Not a
Playboy bunny but an angel. Yeah, that explained it.

Except he didn't want to be dead....

Then Logan realized he was looking at the sky

from a small window. He was flying. In a pretty damn fine helicopter, too.

Oh, boy. Either he really was on his way to heaven, or he was in big trouble.

He'd take door number three instead, thank you very much.

Too bad that didn't appear to be an option.

His hearing was slowly coming back, though everything was sounding tinny and very, very faint, as if coming from miles away. And, damn, the pain had him gasping, wanting to curl into a ball.

Or hurl.

"What's your name?" the angel in scrubs was asking.

"J.T. Logan. Just Logan is good, though," he answered automatically. Which was good, right? It was always good to know your name.

"Okay, J.T. Logan, how many fingers am I holding up?"

Now that stymied him, because, interestingly enough, he didn't see any fingers. Though he did see a lot of that red hair, escaping those messy braids. She had the kind of bangs that swept across her temple and down one side of her face, framing her jaw. Her ears were small, dainty, with two single gold hoops in one ear, and four in the other. Her V-necked scrubs were short-sleeved, revealing toned, tanned arms.

His angel liked to be outside, and she liked to be physical, which in no way took away from the fact that she was nicely stacked.

"How many fingers?" she asked again, bending over him to check one of the pieces of equipment behind him. As she did, her top gaped, revealing a pink bra beneath.

And a heart belly ring.

God bless the belly ring. "Two," he answered definitively, looking at her breasts. "Pink cotton-clad— *ouch!*"

His angel jabbed him with a needle, which answered his question about heaven. He definitely wasn't there. Proving it, she pressed something just behind his ear, which came away bright red.

Blood.

His.

Ah, shit. Pain continued to bloom through him.

"Nice gash there," she said, still frowning. "You'll need stitches after X-rays." Then she set down the blood-soaked cloth and ran her hands down his body, and he wished like hell he could feel them instead of the agony slashing through him because he'd bet her hands were warm and sweet and gentle—

"Besides the possible concussion, I'm going to guess at least two dinged-up ribs—" She paused, probing, while he did his best not to lose his dignity and throw up on her very clean, white athletic shoes. "Make that three."

"That's probably going to hurt pretty good when I stop floating," he said.

Again she leveled him with those green, green eyes. His beautiful, still-frowning flight nurse. "You feel like you're floating?"

"Better than puking, right?" Logan tried a smile and felt his eyes roll in the back of his head at the movement.

"Don't move." She ran her fingers over his ribs and fire burst through his veins instead of blood.

"Holy shit!" he gasped. "What else is injured?"

"I'm guessing some internal bleeding. I think your right leg's fractured. Not sure about your hip."

God. He stared up at the ceiling of the chopper and concentrated on breathing. At least he was breathing. And then it occurred to him that he had no recollection of getting there. "What happened to me?"

"You don't remember?"

He stared at her as his brain hit Pause, Search and then Play. But all he could summon up were the *Playboy* models floating naked on the ocean, pleasuring him however he wanted, when he wanted. Somehow he didn't think she wanted to hear about that.

"It's okay," she said, softening, her fingers touching his jaw. "Just relax, and—"

"Enjoy the flight?" He let out a laugh that definitely wasn't full of amusement. "That depends on what the in-flight movie is for today." Logan went to sit up, and found his vision hampered by yet another explosion of white-hot pain.

"Yeah, that's your ribs. Hence the not moving suggestion."

Got it. Not moving. Very carefully not moving. But as he lay back and went still, he wracked his brain for answers.

None came.

"What's your last memory?" she asked.

"Floating with the bunnies."

She arched that scarred eyebrow. "The fluffy white-tail kind?"

"Um…sure."

She eyed him, and he had a feeling he was slipping nothing by her.

"Huh," she said. "Wonder what *bunnies* were doing at your raid."

"Raid?"

She lifted up the flak vest she'd obviously had to cut off him. The big white letters across the back read *ATF Agent.*

And just like that, it slammed into him. Separating from Hawk on the roof. Hearing Hawk call out Gaines's name. Having it all make terrible gut-wrenching sense and then being hit over the head before being shoved off the roof. It hadn't been Gaines, he'd been on the ground, but one of Gaines's men. He knew it. "Hawk," he said hoarsely. "Where's Hawk?"

His angel/nurse gently set a hand on his chest. Yep, just as he thought, she had a sweet touch. Sweet and unyielding.

Because she wasn't letting him get up.

"My partner," he ground out, gasping as he lay back. "Do you know about him?"

Her eyes filled with compassion as she shook her head. "You're the only one we have tonight."

"Cell phone. I need my—"

"Whoa there, cowboy."

"I need to—"

"Breathe," she said firmly, nodding when he gulped in air. "Yeah, just keep doing that." She was leaning over him again, hands on his upper arms, holding him down. "That's it." She looked behind him to the pilot. "Ethan, ETA?"

"Twelve minutes."

"Almost there," she told Logan, stroking a hand down his arm and back up again, in a manner that was incredibly calming. "You've had quite the night, haven't you?"

"I need to call in—" He broke off at a wave of dizziness. "Shit, this sucks."

"Tell you what. You lie really still for me, and soon as we land, I'll find out about your partner, okay?"

He wanted her to call now. But there were spots swimming in his eyes and he thought maybe he was going to puke after all.

"So, do you remember how you got so dinged up?"

"Took a hit to the head." Which had hurt way more than he'd expected, but not as much as, say, taking a flying leap off a roof. "Then I took a tumble off a roof."

"You fell off a roof?"

"Not fell." His jaw throbbed with tension and all the pain. "I was pushed."

She shook her head. "And I thought *my* job was hazardous."

Logan let out a low laugh, which had him groaning in agony. Again she bent over him.

"Keep breathing," she whispered, eyes on his.

Yeah, he'd keep breathing, soon as he was done throwing up. He would keep breathing, just as long as he could keep looking at her....

HAWK WAS STILL HOLDING ONTO Abby, who was staring in horror at the handcuff on her wrist. He had to admit to feeling a little bit of horror himself, but he had to keep her safe, at all costs. Because that's what he did, he upheld the law, he kept people safe...

And she needed to be kept safe, whether she knew it or not.

God. He'd handcuffed her to him. And somehow he didn't think it would help to explain to her that sometimes to do the right thing you had to cross the line. Especially when he hadn't just crossed it, he'd stomped on it. But, God, she'd tasted so sweet, so hot, he wanted to stomp on that line again....

No. Bad.

Focus.

He was going to keep her safe, at any cost.

The wind had kicked the flames so that they were surrounded, as if in their own, intimate hell. They stared at each other, her glaring, him stunned. Kissing her had been everything he'd ever imagined and more, so much more, because the reality of her willowy body against his had been better than any fantasy. If he hadn't been bleeding all over her from the cut on his head, that is.

Oh, and if he hadn't *cuffed her*. Yeah, that had been the golden touch right there. Really, it was shocking that she wasn't falling all over herself to be with him.

She'd been right after all; he *was* an idiot, and an ass.

Abby tried to jerk free, and she was strong for such a little thing. He hadn't realized that about her. He'd known she was strong-minded, driven, that she enjoyed work, that she had a pair of eyes that cut through all his crap and saw the real him. Oh, and that she'd taken an instant dislike to him from day one.

Under normal circumstances, Hawk might have simply turned up the charm and tried to figure out where he'd taken a wrong step, but Tibbs had warned him way back on her first day to leave her alone. And he had.

Now he was extremely sorry he hadn't cultivated more of a friendship with her regardless because he sure as hell could use her on his side at the moment. Big time.

"Abby, you have to listen to me." Grabbing her shoulders, he backed her to a tree and peered into her face. "You're in danger. We're both in danger. I need you to—"

"Uncuff me."

At the tension in her voice, he eased back. Normally she avoided him like the plague, but she did so with an indifferent disdain that was designed to turn him off, even though for some sick reason it always had the opposite effect.

But there was no disdain now. No, she had a look in those kill-me-slowly baby blues that spelled complete and abject terror.

She really believed him to be the bad guy.

Unbelievable. "Hey. Hey, it's okay. I'm not going to hurt you, I only need to—"

"Let me go, Hawk."

Her fear cut through him and broke his heart. "I can't do that."

"Let. Me. *Go*."

"I hear you, believe me," he said with real regret, protecting her with his body when a blast of wind brought hot ashes drifting down on them. "But I can't do it, I'm sorry."

"Won't, you mean."

"Okay, yeah. Won't. Not until you listen to me."

She glared at him with so much emotion spitting from her eyes, he nearly did as she asked and let go of her. Usually put together, she now had dirt streaked down a cheek and along her jaw, and her shirt was torn. So were her pants, from knees to thigh, exposing one of her world-class legs and the scratches she'd sustained.

She looked like a wreck. A furious, undone, adorable wreck. And he wanted to kiss her again. God, he'd give a limb to do just that.

Scratch that.

He just wanted to hold her. Hold her tight until she was safe, and no longer scared.

Yeah, explain *that*.

"You're a wanted man," she said. "It changes everything, Hawk."

"Wanted for what, exactly?"

"For turning rogue!" Abby arched up with each word, bumping some interesting female body parts into many of his favorite parts. "For running the Kiddie Bombers! For shooting Gaines! Pick one!"

"I would, except for one thing. I am not running the Kiddie Bombers."

"But I saw you shoot him." Her voice quavered though her eyes did not. Nope, they were cemented to his, shiny with emotion and a self-righteousness, which normally made him want to wrestle her down and mess up her hair and wrinkle her clothes.

But she was already ruffled, which was just as well because he couldn't summon even a shred of playfulness or his legendary calm, not with his heart lodged in his throat. "You have to trust me," he said quietly.

She stared at him, then slowly shook her head.

Fine. *Christ.* Hawk was not a man used to explaining himself, but he gave it a go now, he had to. "Okay, I shot him, yes."

"Oh, my God."

"But it was in self-defense. This was all a crazy setup. Gaines has been running the Kiddie Bombers. He's been re-selling the confiscated weapons, putting them back on the streets, probably at a pretty profit. But I got too close, and now I've become a problem to him. He decided to lay the blame on me and then fake his death."

She stared at him like he'd lost it, and truthfully—he had. He totally had. "He's still very much alive, Abby. I didn't kill him, I swear it."

He didn't realize how much he needed her to believe him until she stared up at his face, her heart in her eyes.

"I know," she whispered. "He can't be dead because he called me."

"He *what?*"

"He wanted to tell me you were the bad guy." She stared down at the handcuff linking them.

"I'm not," he promised. "But he's feeling closed in by all the loose ends now." He touched her face. "You're a loose end, Ab. You're in danger. He means for me to die here tonight, and now, I think he means the same for you. Please, let's not let him win."

Abby swept her gaze down the length of him, and he knew what she saw. Blood. His. Gaines's. "I swear it," he whispered. "I won't hurt you."

"Then uncuff me."

"Do you promise to come with me, so I can keep you safe?"

"I'm not ready to promise you anything."

This evening was not going his way. "Where's Logan?"

"He was air-lifted out."

That stopped Hawk cold. "What? What happened?"

"He fell from the barn roof."

Christ. "Listen to me," he said, gripping her shoulders and giving her a little shake. "Logan didn't fall from any roof, he would never have fallen. Don't you get it? He's fucking with us, Abby, like we're toys."

"Then come in with me, and we'll figure this all out."

"By *in,* you mean turn myself in?"

It was all over her face, and he shook his head. "Hawk—"

"I need to get to Logan, wherever they took him. He's in danger, too."

"Fine. After we go back, we'll—"

"No." He laughed harshly. "Let me save you some bullshitting time, okay? I overheard you and Watkins. If I go in, I go in charged for Gaines's murder. Even though you and I both know he's not dead."

He watched her eyes once again lock on the blood splattered down the front of his shirt. Watched as she stepped close to set her hand on him. The warmth from her body seeped right through to his chilled flesh, and he nearly shut his eyes, but then he realized she'd slipped that hand around him, reaching for the rifle he'd swiped from her.

That settled it.

Time for Plan B. And though his muscles screamed in protest, and every inch of him hurt like hell, he pressed her back against the tree. "Don't even think about it." Before she could find another way to kill him, he took off running, forcing her along with him.

"Hey!" Abby tugged, trying to slow him down.

"Later." He'd talk her into believing him later. He'd have to. "We're going on the run. Together."

7

WITH LITTLE CHOICE, ABBY FOUND herself racing alongside Hawk, whose endurance showed her she'd been stupid to think she could ever win in a physical battle with him—and, given that she'd put herself in a position to be caught and handcuffed, possibly not even a battle of wits. They dodged through trees, the heat of the fire following them. Everything seemed to be engulfed. Flames flickered and hissed and snapped all around them.

She wondered if the farmhouse had caught fire as well, wondered if the others were looking for her, wondered about Elliot. "Where are you taking me?"

"To get to the bottom of this unbelievably fucked-up night."

She tried to slow him down and came up against the restraint of the handcuffs, which reminded her. She had a panic attack scheduled for, oh, right about *now*. "I can't be handcuffed, Hawk," she puffed. "I can't—"

"Just run."

"See, that's the thing." She gasped for breath. "You're just making this worse on yourself—"

"Shh."

He stopped so fast Abby blinked. She eyed the veins in his temples working overtime. His jaw was so tight it could shatter. "Do you realize you've spoken more words to me in the past sixty seconds than in our entire relationship?"

"I need to know what's going on, Hawk. Now."

"I told you. The Kiddie Bombers have been run by an inside mole all along. Gaines. And I've apparently gotten too close. He's got no choice now but to stop me. And Logan. And you, Abby."

The situation was impossible, not real, and yet...

And yet his words reminded her that over a year ago, she'd also been suspicious about how the group seemed to know the ATF's every step. Then she'd been kidnapped, and had ended up being distracted by the events of that whole nightmare night, and then her rescue and leave of absence.

"Come on," Hawk urged. "He's not working alone, there are others. We have to get out of here."

The next thing she knew they were running again, through the trees, far from the fire, from the scene. "Hawk."

Ignoring her, he just kept pulling her along, and when she dragged her feet, he simply entwined his fingers in hers and tugged harder.

"Stop." Accompanying this demand, she dug her heels into the ground, but it was frozen and slippery, and all she did was trip.

"Jesus." The hands he put on her waist felt strong

and very capable as he steadied her. She'd set something off in him, and if she wasn't mistaken, it was concern, not anger. "Don't be stupid."

"I'm not going anywhere with you, Hawk. Except back to the others. Now uncuff me." She nearly choked on her next word but spit it out anyway. *"Please."*

Hearing the crack in her voice, he grimaced, and so did she. *Oh, God. Don't be pathetic, Abby. Keep it together.*

"We both know what will happen to me if we go back," he said. "I'm being set up, Abby. And by the time the red tape gets untangled, it'll be too late. Gaines will be gone."

"Gone? Where?"

"Who knows. Some uncharted South Pacific island. But not before he makes us pay."

"You're wrong." Her chest felt tight. God, who to believe? "He wouldn't hurt me."

He let out a frustrated breath and gave her a little shake. "Why are you so loyal to him? What does he have over you?"

He'd saved her, and she'd never be able to forget that. "I owe him…everything."

Hawk stared at her for a long moment, opened his mouth, then closed it. "This is crazy, you know that? Gaines is after us, I swear it."

"And your proof of all this is…?"

Behind them came the sound of a man's shout.

"Shit. Run," he commanded.

"Hawk—"

He pulled her along. "My gut is screaming," he told her over his shoulder. "And my gut is never, ever wrong."

"But—"

"Jesus. Can't you just trust me?"

"No!" She was panting for air. "Because you're basing all this on your gut. That's not enough."

"Yes, I—" He took one glance at her undoubtedly mutinous expression and shook his head. "Ah, forget it." Ruthlessly he continued to pull her along, on a path only he knew.

So much was wrong, Abby couldn't even wrap her mind around the facts, or her feet, apparently, because she tripped again. She'd have landed flat on her face, too, if Hawk hadn't grabbed her at the cost of his own balance, and then they were falling anyway, hitting the cold ground. As luck would have it, her chin bounced off a patch of snow instead of dirt, which she supposed she should appreciate.

"Shit." Hawk was on all fours, head down, breathing hard. *"Shit!"*

"Yeah, you've already said that."

Turning his head, he leveled her with an extremely unamused glare. "If you could keep in mind we're attached."

"If you could keep in mind that you're kidnapping me!"

"I'm *protecting* you!"

"Then uncuff me." She was breathing as if they'd been running miles, instead of a quarter mile, tops, but she needed to be uncuffed. *Now.* "You don't need me," she gasped. "Just uncuff me and go do what you've got to do."

"You have to stay with me. Or—"

"Or what? Or I'll be safe?"

"Damn it, I told you, *I'm* keeping you safe!"

"Let me go." She heard the panic in her voice but couldn't help it. "I'm…I'm begging you, Hawk."

He closed his eyes. "Abby…" His voice was hoarse. "I have to do this. If something happens to you, I won't be able to live with myself."

"Nothing's going to happen to me—"

"Right, because I'm going to make sure of it. Besides, I know you. If I let you go, you'll go digging—"

"No." He didn't know her. He didn't know, for example, that she was an inch from meltdown. Or that she could scarcely breathe because of it. Or that she didn't understand any of this, not the way she'd broken protocol and left the van in the first place to run after him when she'd thought him in danger, not the way she'd let him kiss her for a good long time before she'd kneed him…

And now she was handcuffed to him, the man she'd been so secretly attracted to. Gee, what great taste she had. Clearly there was something seriously wrong with her. "So you want me to believe that this is for *my* protection?"

"Yes," he said, clearly relieved that she got it.

But all she got was that he was unbelievable. "What an overprotective, egomaniacal, stupid thing to do! I can protect myself, Hawk. My God, I'm a trained agent, too!"

He was already shaking his head, his eyes flat and stubborn. "No. You didn't see him tonight. You didn't see his eyes." He turned from her and studied the night. "He's lost it. Completely."

Abby tried to see whatever he was looking at, but she couldn't see a thing. She had no idea how he decided which way to go, but suddenly they were moving through the woods again. As they moved, she eyed his pockets, wondering which one held the key for the cuffs.

Because she was going to get free.

The wind continued to whip at them, cutting bites that nipped at her skin. The smoke was still thick, choking her. When she started coughing, Hawk stopped and waited for her to catch her breath.

A thoughtful captor. Too bad she still wanted to kill him.

He wasn't looking at her now, but was taking in their surroundings, an awareness about him, a physical readiness. He was primed and ready for more trouble, but then he turned to her, and his eyes changed. Softened. He pulled something from her hair. And something else. Twigs, she imagined. Pine needles.

Then he touched her face.

She jerked back at the uncomfortable, unfortunately familiar, claustrophobic feeling of someone being too close. "Don't."

Don't touch me.

It was too dark to see his expression clearly, but he went still for a charged moment, then stepped back as far as he could, considering they were still linked. "I told you, I'm not going to hurt you."

But that wasn't the promise she wanted. "So let me go."

Instead, he turned away. "Let's go. Almost there." And they were running again.

From the depths of her pocket, Abby felt her cell phone vibrate. Incoming text message. She glanced at Hawk. He was slightly ahead of her, watching where they were going. That, and the dark night allowed her to pull out her cell without his seeing. She flicked aside the mini credit card attached to the small chain on the antennae in order to see the screen. Watkins. Where are you?

She hit Reply, then hesitated because there was the little issue of trust. She had no idea who to believe. Abby shook her head. *No.* That didn't matter right now, all that mattered was getting free. She hit Send, and off the blank message went. As an SOS. It would have to do.

They came to a clearing that she recognized. They'd gone in one big circle, eastbound, putting them just south of the farmhouse…. She looked around but saw nothing with which to help herself. The woods were thick, black as the inside of Hawk's heart, but still not as scary as, say, being handcuffed to him.

Damn, she wished she had her rifle back. She'd get that, too, along with the key. She was determined.

And terrified.

She tried to keep the panic at bay. After all, tonight was nothing, nothing at all, like her nightmare.

The nightmare that had really happened.

First of all, it'd been daytime, at a gun specialty shop where it'd been suspected the Kiddie Bombers were selling confiscated weapons out of the back. She'd been on duty the day of the raid. In hindsight, it had been just rotten luck. Not so agreeable to the raid, the men had fought back as if they'd known the ATF were coming. Abby had been taken hostage and held in a basement, a cold, dark, dank place that even now, a year later, she could still smell in her dreams.

"I thought you were hurt," she said bitterly to Hawk's back, forced to keep her feet moving or get dragged along.

"Just stunned."

"From?"

"Taking a bullet to the chest." Slowing to a walk, he grabbed her free hand and pressed it up against his vest, over his heart, forcing her to feel the hole in his vest.

A bullet indentation. "He shot you when you pulled your gun on him?"

"No. He shot me point-blank."

"He must have known you were wearing a vest. Why didn't he shoot you where he'd have had a chance at killing you?"

"He tried. But it was dark, and I rolled. Then I pulled a gun on him."

"That's not what I saw."

"Sweetheart, I am not trying to argue with you here, but maybe you should get your eyes checked."

"You're saying Elliot drew on you first?"

"Elliot?" Hawk asked, and stopped so unexpectedly that she plowed into the back of him. "You call him Elliot?"

"It's his name."

"Sounds pretty chummy."

Yes, well, after he'd busted into that basement, guns drawn, to find her stripped naked and staring down the thugs who'd just pulled out a set of jumper cables to torture her with, they were definitely on a first-name basis. "We have a…history."

Hawk just stared at her, his eyes gleaming in the night. Clearly this news had not made his day. "So, you were what, fucking the boss while he was stealing back the confiscated stolen weapons to re-sell them on the black market?"

"You really are an asshole."

"Just calling it like I see it."

"You don't know what you're talking about."

"No? Then enlighten me."

Abby pressed the fingers of her free hand to her eyes and tried to keep a level head. "Why? Why would he do such things, Hawk?"

"Well, connecting the dots, I'd hazard a guess that it's because he's the bad guy."

Rolling her eyes, she turned away.

He sighed and pulled her back. "You want me to believe that lover boy never mentioned any of this when you two were doing the tangle on his sheets?"

Staring up at him, she slowly shook her head, feeling frustration and anger push aside her fear. Good, because she'd sure as hell rather be pissed off than afraid. "You are way out of line, Hawk."

"Yeah? Then put me in line." He stood there, his eyes searching hers, not mocking now, just wanting the truth.

But she didn't have the words. "Just tell me what you think we're supposed to do now."

"We need proof of Gaines's indiscretions. Unfortunately, my rock-solid proof ran off."

"What?"

"Eighteen months ago I shot the leader of the Kiddie Bombers. It was dark, in a warehouse, but I got him. Tonight, wrestling with Gaines, I saw the scar. Here." He pointed to his collarbone.

"A bullet hole? But lots of ATF agents have bullet holes."

"Not undocumented ones. But now we have this." He patted the rifle. "If the serial number on this baby matches one of the serial numbers on the ATF database, it's one of the pieces of the puzzle."

Her mind whirled. "But even if that matches—"

"Yeah, yeah, we still need to tie it to Gaines, I know."

"*If* it's him."

"Abby—"

"Because from where I'm standing…" She jangled the cuffs. "It sure as hell could still be you."

She waited for him to defend himself, and though a muscle bunched in his jaw, he said nothing.

"I'm not going to make this easy for you," she told him.

Rubbing a weary hand over his face, Hawk sighed. "Yeah. Tell me something I don't know."

8

"Keep moving," Hawk demanded, refusing to give in to Abby's resistance when he was this close. They were headed toward the farmhouse and the trucks he'd seen there. His plan—get to an ATF database.

"Damn it, Hawk. Slow down."

She was tugging again and probably going to yank them to the ground, which she'd done four times and counting. He had the bloody knees to prove it, which, considering how dead Gaines wanted him, was the least of his worries.

Jesus, he could hardly even wrap his brain around how badly the evening had gone. Logan, down. Gaines, rogue. Abby...definitely not on his side.

He wasn't sure whose side that put her on.

"Hawk."

He'd been trying to ignore her, but she sounded panicked and breathless. Not from running so much as hyperventilating, and while that fact brought out some sympathy, it also came with annoyance, because, for Christ's sake, he wasn't hurting her.

He'd never hurt her.

Too bad she wouldn't say the same. "Nearly there."

To her credit, she kept going, but he knew it wasn't for him but to get to wherever he was headed and get uncuffed. He appreciated the warrior in her, more than she could know, because his shoulder blades kept itching.

Gaines was out there, armed, gunning for them.

They had to keep moving.

At the edge of the woods, he finally came to a stop. Abby stood as far away as the restraints would allow, so that the chain was pulled taut and the metal was digging into his raw skin. She had to feel it, too, but apparently she refused to even breathe in the same vicinity as him.

Good to know tonight was no different from any other.

He could see the faint outline of the farmhouse that he'd circled around to, and just behind that was a handful of cars. All ripe for the picking because, as he now knew, tonight had been nothing more than a setup.

Which meant he should be able to commandeer one of those vehicles and get them the hell out of there. Exactly *where* he would get them the hell *to* was yet to be determined, but one thing was clear— he couldn't let himself be brought in. Not until he could prove his innocence and Gaines's guilt.

"I think the truck is our best bet."

Abby was breathing harshly but not fighting him, which was an unexpected bonus. She had more twigs in her hair and a nasty scratch on one cheek. Her clothes were torn and beyond dirty from wrestling on the ground with him. She'd started the day so neat, too.

Just looking at her had something inside him softening. In a different time and place, he'd have reached over and pulled her close, maybe burying his face in her hair, pressing his mouth to her skin…

But her attention was on the cuffs, as if she could remove them by glare alone. He wished she'd just let it go for now, but she was definitely not the letting go type. "Keep up, okay?"

"I have a better plan. Uncuff me."

"I can't."

"Won't, you mean."

"Okay, won't. You'll turn me in before I can prove I'm right."

"You know what? Don't talk to me."

Oh, good. She was definitely coming around, surrendering to his charms. "See that truck?" he asked. "We're going for that."

Taking that whole not-talking-to-him thing pretty seriously, she didn't answer. But she was looking at him plenty, sending icy stares that felt like daggers. Probably trying to decide how to murder him, slowly. Resigned, Hawk pulled her toward the fifteen-year-old Ford pickup painted a combo of forest-green and bad-weather rust. He pulled open the driver's door, which was blessedly unlocked. Putting his hands on Abby's waist, he bent at the knees to hoist her in ahead of him.

She balked. Of course she balked, but he didn't have time for this. Now that they were clear of the fire and the chaos, the night was quiet, *too* quiet, making him extremely uneasy.

"I vote we go back to the van," she said.

He shook his head.

"I'm not getting into this truck with you."

She was tired. Scared. He got that. But that would have to be taken care of later, say if they lived, so to that end, he pressed his body into hers, trying to get her inside the cab of the truck. Her hair jabbed him in the eyes, her ass ground into his crotch, neither of which was exactly an unpleasant sensation, but at the contact, she jerked as if shot and jumped away from him, pulling on the cuffs.

"Jesus, Abby. Just do this. *Please.* Just get in."

"Uncuff me."

"Soon as we're out of here, I swear. I have to jump-start it."

"Oh, God." She hunched over, covering her face with her free hand, breathing like a lunatic.

What the hell? He touched her shoulder, and she nearly leapt out of her skin, eyes wide. Wild. Like she was no longer with him.

"Hey." Hawk lifted his free hand and wondered what was going on. "Hey, it's just me."

Her hysterical laugh broke the silence. Up until right then, a part of him, admittedly a sick part, had been enjoying their close contact, the way her body fit to his, the scent of her hair, how when he'd tried to lift her into the truck, her breasts had pressed into his forearm. But this reaction from her, this genuine fear, made him feel like a molester. "I'm not going to hurt you, Abby. I swear it. Just get into the truck, and I'll—"

"No!"

He understood her reticence, he really did, but she'd screamed this, leaving him no choice but to slide his hand over her mouth.

Of course, because this was Abby, she bit him, and then she was fighting him like a feral cat, tooth and nail. She fought dirty, too, twisting his arm but good as she whirled and tried to punch him in the throat, instead catching him high on his bruised chest, which hurt enough to have him chomping down on both his lip and his frustration. "Abby, stop. I am *not* the bad guy!"

She stopped fighting and brought her head up, eyes still wide but not so wild. "I swear it," he whispered, smoothing his fingers along the curve of her jaw. He had no idea when his priorities this night had changed from kicking Gaines's ass to seeing this woman safe, but they had. "It's going to be okay—"

Another harsh laugh, this one a half sob, and she yanked at their joined wrists so hard his teeth grated. He began to understand something he'd missed before in the rush to survive—she definitely had something else going on here, something that the handcuffs were only making worse.

But it would have to wait, because for now he had to get out of here before he was discovered, and she was coming with him, period. To that end, Hawk bodily lifted her into the truck, taking another kick to the thigh in the process, swearing as he bent beneath the console to hot-wire the car.

"Hot-wire," she gasped, still breathless from the fight, as the engine leaped to life. "Not jump."

"Right."

"You said jump."

Had he? "To jump-start it, I'd have needed another car."

"And cables."

"Yes." It was the way she said *cables* that had him trying to get a look at her face as he whipped the truck around. But she turned her head away, staring out the window into the dark night.

Exhausted, but pumped full of adrenaline, he headed down the road without lights, driving slowly enough to avoid kicking up dust, but hopefully fast enough that no one noticed them. The road was completely deserted, but he didn't breathe freely until the main highway. There he flicked on the headlights and hit the gas. He was aware of Abby sitting stiffly, as far from him as she could get, her hand dangling limply near the steering wheel.

Saying nothing.

There weren't many cars on the highway this late at night. Hell, there were *no* cars. Out here, even the wide-open spaces had wide-open spaces.

In the daylight the view had been of wildflower meadows, fall foliage and towering peaks all around them, covered in deep forests.

But at night, the sky-scratching mountains were no more than a dark looming outline, creating a feeling of vastness, which only increased his sense of isolation.

It was many moments before they saw another vehicle, and then, in the oncoming headlights, Hawk glanced over at Abby.

She hadn't relaxed, not a single muscle. Her skin

was pale, her hair wild around her face, her eyes huge and underlined with exhaustion. "Abby," he said softly.

No answer, big surprise.

"I realize you're pissed and probably going to castrate me at the first opportunity, but before you do, just tell me one thing."

Her eyes cut to his.

"What happened to you?"

She closed those eyes.

And his heart sunk, because he'd gotten the answer to his next question. Whatever it'd been, it'd been bad, very bad. And it wasn't hard to make a few educated guesses, none of which he wanted to think about her suffering through.

Abby didn't speak, just sat there silently stewing. Steam practically rose from her clothing, which was even more ripped and dirty now and made him feel like crap because he'd done this to her.

Shooting him another sidelong glance that had his death written all over it, she hugged herself with her one free arm, took a deep breath as if steeling herself against the craziness they'd left behind and what was to come, and thrust her chin to nose-bleed heights.

While Hawk loved the show of bravado, he knew no one could maintain it for long, and when she crashed, that would be his fault, too.

When she finally spoke, it wasn't what he expected. "You're on empty."

He looked at her, surprised she cared enough to

notice. "I know. Believe me, I could sleep for at least a week—"

"The gas tank."

"What?" He looked at the gauge and thought, *ah, shit.* Just one more thing in a long list of things that were not going his way tonight.

9

Somewhere south of Bullet City, Wyoming

WAS IT GOOD OR BAD THAT THEY found a gas station almost immediately? Abby couldn't decide as Hawk pulled the truck off the highway and into the parking lot. From her perch in the passenger seat, she searched for an attendant, a customer, anyone she could flag down for help.

But there was not a single soul.

The handcuffs clanked as Hawk shifted, and her hand brushed his, making her breath hitch. She was so used to avoiding a man's touch, she found herself startled by the fact that though she was still furious, she was not afraid of their close proximity.

Why was Hawk different from other men?

Didn't matter. Slipping her free hand into her pants pocket, she closed her fingers around her cell phone. Hawk was looking at the pump, his head turned from her. Now or never, she decided…

Thumbing open the phone, Abby tried to figure out who to call, then froze as her finger inadvertently pushed a key.

At the unmistakable electronic beep, Hawk's head whipped back to hers. "What was that?"

She shrugged.

"Goddamnit." Pressing her back against the door, he set his hand low on her ribs.

"Hey!"

But his hand merely slid further down, brushing her hip, inching into her pocket without qualm, his fingers closing over hers. "What are you doing?"

Momentarily stunned at how intimate it felt to have his fingers in her pocket, so close to her, with his big body holding her prone against the seat, it took her a moment to answer. "Nothing."

"Doesn't feel like nothing."

Nope. It felt like…like he had his hand down her pants. "I'm just keeping my hand warm." It was amazing how fast the lie rolled off her tongue.

It would have been better if she hadn't sounded so damn breathless.

In answer, he slid his thumb over her lower lip. "Did you text someone?"

She licked her lips, the tip of her tongue accidentally touching his thumb. In response, he inhaled unevenly, and as if connected to him, her stomach quivered.

"Abby? Did you?"

"Uh…" For some odd reason, she'd lost track of the conversation.

"Did you tell anyone where we are?"

Needing him to get off her, she rocked up, managing only to bump her hips to his. He was surrounding her, holding her down, and it left her feeling confused, muddled. Instead of fighting him, as she'd figured she would, her body was doing a sort of slow-burning awareness thing, complete with hard nipples and quivering thighs. *What the hell?*

Hawk didn't appear outwardly affected by their closeness at all. Instead, he kept track of the issue at hand with apparent ease.

Why couldn't she keep track of the issue at hand?

"Did you?" he demanded, then pulled out the phone himself. When he swore, she assumed he'd located her blank text message in the sent file.

Shutting the phone, he lifted his head. Their mouths were a fraction of an inch apart, and somehow fascinated by this, she stared at his lips.

"You lied," he said very softly.

"No."

Honestly, she had no idea why she kept lying. He had the proof in his hand. "I—"

"Stop." As if to insure she did just that, he covered her mouth with his.

This time, this second kiss, Abby didn't have to brace herself. She knew what to expect, an inexplicable onslaught of hunger and desire, so compelling that a low sigh fell from her.

At the sound, he went utterly still, then slid his free hand into her hair, tightening his grip, changing the angle of the kiss to better suit him as he ran his tongue along her lower lip.

Oh, God. Two things occurred simultaneously. One, her heart skittered into near cardiac arrest, and two…a horrifyingly needy moan escaped her.

Hawk pulled back. Though his lids were heavy over his eyes so that she couldn't get a read from them, she sensed his confusion matched hers. "I must be insane," he whispered. "Totally and completely insane."

Yeah, no argument there.

"Tell me again you're not in on this whole thing," he whispered, still holding her face. "Because if you are, you should just kill me now."

"You're crazy."

"Please answer."

Slowly she shook her head.

"Is that no, you're not going to answer, or no—"

"No, I'm not in on this whole thing."

He stared at her for a beat, then let out a breath as he levered himself up off her. "Okay. Okay, that's going to have to be good enough, isn't it? Come on, we're getting out."

She turned to the windshield and was shocked to find it fogged up, dripping condensation. Had they done that? Steamed up the glass with just a simple kiss? Except there'd been nothing simple about it at all…. "We'll freeze to death."

"Can't freeze to death in hell, and I'm definitely in hell." Sitting back, he shoved his free hand through his short hair, making it stand on end. His eyes were shadowed, his lean jaw scruffy, his clothes tattered and blood-strewn. The cut on his forehead had stopped bleeding, but she guessed from his uneven breathing that he still hurt pretty good.

She should be glad. Instead, all Abby felt was a sense of uneasiness, and—truthfully?—a secret wish that he'd go back to holding her. Because for some reason, in his arms she'd felt safer than she had in a very long time.

HAWK EYED THE GAS STATION. It was quiet and badly lit. Both things worked in their favor, or so he hoped.

But it'd only been an hour since the first explosion. Gaines's men couldn't be far behind them. "They'll have figured out you're missing by now. And we know they're looking for me."

Nothing from the woman cuffed to him.

"We'll have to hurry."

She raised an eyebrow, and wordlessly offered up her wrist to be uncuffed.

He had no right to continue to hold her to him, he had nothing but a gut instinct that said he'd saved her life. The best thing now was to get her to Tibbs. Tibbs would keep her safe.

But the thought of walking away from her killed him, though he had no idea why.

Okay, he knew why. He knew exactly why. It was her eyes, mirrors to his own soul. It was the way she brought something out in him, the best part.

And having her smoking body so close to his didn't hurt…. Clearly, kissing her had destroyed too many brain cells. "You're going to run screaming the moment I uncuff you."

More of her loaded nothing.

"Look, I took you with me for your own good—"

She let out a snort that managed to perfectly convey exactly how full of shit she thought he was.

"Jesus." He pinched the bridge of his nose. "I'm a lot of things, Abby, I'll give you that. Stubborn. Tough. Maybe even as asshole—"

She nodded in agreement, which worked wonders for his ego, it really did.

"But whatever you think of me," he insisted. "I'm not a liar."

She slanted him a baleful stare.

"Okay, name it," he challenged her. "Name a lie I've told."

Clearly unable to, she turned her head away.

"Okay, fine. Great. Don't talk to me. Just promise me that you won't scream for help." He unzipped a small pocket on his outer thigh, pulling out a key. "Promise me, and I'll uncuff you."

At that, she leveled him with a furious look. "So now you *want* me to lie?"

"Fine." He tucked the key away again. "We'll do this the hard way. Why the fuck not? We've done everything else that way all damn night."

She went back to her stony silence, and he was back to talking to himself. "I'm going to slide out. You're going to sit in the driver's seat and give me as much slack as you can while I pump gas."

She didn't answer, big surprise. He reached for the door, then let out a breath at the renewed pain in his chest.

Abby looked at him, her gaze darkening with what he sincerely hoped was a tiny bit of sympathy. Some of her hair had slipped free of its bond, falling in silken curves around her face, framing those eyes he could look at all day.

"The effects shouldn't last much longer," she said.

He wasn't sure why, but something turned over inside of him, and it was all he could do not to haul her close and kiss her again, just hold onto her until this nightmare was over. Except she was sending out serious back-off signals, so he got out of the driver's seat to get the gas. She willingly shifted over, giving him enough arm room to maneuver the nozzle into the gas tank.

And that's when he remembered. He had no money.

His gaze locked with hers, and he could see she'd thought of the same thing, since her eyes were mocking him. Christ, he was tired of fighting with her. "You don't by any chance have a wallet on you?"

She simply arched an eyebrow.

Terrific. He hadn't died of smoke inhalation, his wounds, or the fact that his heart had been ripped out by everyone believing he'd gone rogue. Nope, he was going to die because he'd been stupid enough to take her with him, to protect her no less, when she'd as soon rip off his nuts. "Do you or do you not have any money?"

"I don't carry money when I'm being kidnapped."

Hawk understood her anger, he really did. But he was hurting, too, and cold, and just about beyond frustrated. "He's coming for you, too, Abby."

She turned her head to lock her gaze on his. As she did, the scent of her hair drifted over him like a sweet balm. He had no time to be feeling anything since he was currently up hell's creek without a paddle. And yet he felt plenty, mostly an inexplicable need to kiss her again. "I need your cell phone."

"No. Don't—" She choked as his fingers slid across her abdomen, trying to get to her pocket. "Don't touch me."

"Relax." His hand brushed the warm skin of her belly just above her low waistband. "I only want the—"

Her elbow clocked him in the nose, and he saw stars. "Jesus!" He fell back against the opened door. "Jesus Christ, woman!"

Breathing like a lunatic, she glared at him, eyes hot and furious beneath the hair that had fallen in her face. "I told you not to touch."

"Okay, yeah, getting that loud and clear. The phone, Abby."

Her jaw tightened. "It's almost out of battery."

The battery didn't matter, and they both knew it. She threw her cellphone at him, and thank you, God, the little keychain he'd seen with her mini credit card was attached to it.

"I can't believe you expect your victim to pay for your gas."

"No, what I expect is to wake up from this nightmare any second, but I'm not going to get that lucky." He swiped the card at the pump and nearly fell to his knees in gratitude when the gas began pumping into the truck.

Her cell phone vibrated in his hand. Incoming

text message. His gaze locked with hers, then he looked at the caller ID. "Do you know this number?"

She looked and blinked.

"Abby?"

"It's an established line between Gaines and me. He got it after…it was just for us to communicate back and forth."

He flipped open the phone to read: Where are you?

"Interesting that he isn't concerned with making you think he's dead. Interesting, and very telling."

"Right." She closed her eyes. "Because if I'm on his short list for the evening, it doesn't matter if I know he's alive. Because I won't be for much longer." She slid him a glance that sliced at his heart as she waited for him to nod.

Hawk slapped the phone closed against his thigh and sighed.

She didn't say anything more, and after a moment he realized she wasn't being obstinate—her default mood of the night—but rather trying hard to control whatever emotion she was keeping to herself. Bending closer, he risked life and limb to see into her face. "Talk to me."

She just shook her head.

"Abby—"

"Please," she whispered, clearly trying with all her might to keep it together. "Don't. Just let me think."

Okay. He could do that. For a little while, anyway. But then she shifted in the seat at the same time he pulled back, and her shoulder brushed his chest. The accidental touch seemed to freeze her.

It sure as hell froze him, and he watched as very slowly her head came up. God, her eyes, they completely slayed him. He just wanted to look at her all night. Look at her and inhale her and touch her.... The yearning was nothing new. He'd been inhaling deeply to catch her scent for six long months now. Hawk breathed her in and tried not to lose it, but, God, she got him, right in the gut.

In the heart.

She had a strand of silky hair over one eye, and very, very slowly he reached out to stroke it away, wanting to do much more but unable to figure out how to further touch her without her gutting him. "It's going to be okay," he murmured. "Unfortunately, I don't know exactly how, but we'll get there, I promise."

Her gaze searched his, soft now, uncertain, leaving him just as uncertain what to make of the shadowed expression in her eyes. Was she still mad? Hurt? Was she feeling any of what he was feeling, which was that he wanted to kiss her again, for real this time, without anything coming between them?

Abby turned away.

And there was his answer. No, she was not feeling any of what he was. Still waiting on the gas, he pulled out the phone again and dialed Logan's cell. No answer. Damn... Glancing up, he found her watching him.

"Last I heard," she said quietly. "He was in the air, headed back to Cheyenne County."

He only hoped that wasn't as serious as it sounded. "Okay, so we go with what we've got. The rifle. I just have to match it to the ATF serial number list to place it as one of the stolen weapons. So we need to get into regional offices."

"Or to my laptop at home."

"Yeah, much easier. Let's go."

"There's that 'let's' again."

"We have to do this, Abby. Placing the rifle is evidence of the inside job."

"Still not enough."

"Well, we'll think of more then. We have to do this, you know we do."

"No, we don't. *We* don't have to do anything." But Hawk realized the heat in her voice was gone.

Best news all night, from where he stood, because whether she knew it or not, he was winning her over. "If I'm wrong, I'll—"

"What? Turn yourself in?"

"Yeah."

She stared at him. "Let's call Tibbs now."

"Not without the serial number. Not when he already has evidence against me."

"Hawk…"

"Look, if I'm wrong, you can call him. I promise."

She tugged on the cuffs. "Your promise is no good to me when I'm with you against my will."

Okay, good point. But he wasn't letting her go until they were back on the road, because he wasn't going to risk her getting out of the truck this close to Gaines. "I'm sorry."

"If that were true, I wouldn't be here."

"No, I'm sorry about whatever happened to you."

Abby went so still he doubted she was even breathing. Slowly she lifted her gaze to meet his, and then *he* wasn't breathing, because there, revealed for him to see, was such pain he nearly staggered backward.

In the loaded silence came the startlingly loud click of the gas pump, signaling that the tank was full, and she blinked and turned away.

Moment over.

By the time Hawk got back into the truck, with her hurriedly scooting over so that he wouldn't have to touch her, she'd regained her control.

And reestablished her silence.

He started the engine, but she cleared her throat and rattled the handcuffs.

Right. Hoping he wasn't being an idiot, he pulled out onto the highway before he tossed the key into her lap. She wouldn't do anything stupid at sixty-five miles per hour, he figured.

Hoped.

Abby grabbed the key. Bending her head, she set herself to the task of unlocking the cuffs, her hair falling over his forearm, her breasts inadvertently brushing his bicep. She'd probably have a heart attack if she realized but he had another reaction altogether.

Freed, she rubbed her wrist and stared out the window. Reaching over, he brought her hand close until he could see her skin in the dim light of the console display. She was bruised, abraded and raw.

"Don't you dare say you're sorry," she told him.

He closed his lips on the words and pressed his lips to her skin.

She didn't snatch her hand free, which he considered an excellent sign. Instead, her breath caught as if maybe she liked his touch after all, as if maybe she was finally going to surrender her aggression and fear, and soften toward him. At least in his dreams.

"Why would he show himself to you?"

His eyes met hers. So she hadn't decided that he was completely full of shit. He'd take that. "I think it was sheer cockiness, to tell you the truth. Sort of like, look what I pulled off."

"But to play both sides… It's so crazy dangerous."

"He's dying tonight, remember," he reminded her. "In essence, retiring."

"After getting rid of his loose ends."

"Yes."

"Like you."

"Yes."

She nodded, clearly holding it together by a string, and he wanted to touch her so badly, just to let her know she wasn't alone.

"I keep going back," she said. "To when I was working on the Kiddie Bombers in Seattle."

He slanted her a glance. "Something clicking?"

"There were several times when things went down like tonight, when Gaines showed up at raids no one expected him to be at. To watch the takedowns, he always said." She shook her head. "Once I questioned him on that."

"And he was thrilled."

"He brushed me off." Abby shook her head. "And I let him. I discounted all of it until now. But I'm thinking that on the off chance I was getting too close…" She closed her eyes. "I'm a loose end, too."

"Yes, but you're an alive one," he reminded her. "Let's keep it that way. First, your computer."

"And then what? We draw him out in order to prove he's alive?"

It was the first real sign he'd had that she might believe him. "I like the way you think, and yeah. He needs to be drawn out."

Which Hawk would do alone, because no way in hell did he plan on letting Gaines anywhere near her. In fact, he needed to find a safe place for her until this was over. And yet…and yet there was a small part of him that couldn't deny what it felt like having her with him.

Because with her here, he wasn't alone. As disastrously bad as the night had gone, as bad as it could still get, he wasn't alone.

10

LOGAN WOKE UP IN A WHITE ROOM filled with beeping equipment and a sterile smell that made him groan in disgust.

A hospital.

He hated hospitals, always had. His asshole father had put him in several, until the state had finally decided, oh, gee, maybe we'd better do our job and remove the kid from his situation. Logan had thrived in foster homes, but thanks in no small part to his wild streak, he'd still managed to land himself in various emergency rooms all on his own.

Then there'd been Special Forces and the time he and Hawk had been nearly shot to kingdom come when their convoy had been hit in the Gulf.

Since then, however, he'd actually managed to stay hospital free, though he had a running bet with Hawk—one hundred bucks on which of them would run out of luck first.

And damn it, now he'd lost. Unless he could get himself checked out before Hawk found out....

Something rustled at his side, and a face swam in front of his. Fiery red hair, black-rimmed glasses, mossy eyes and well-glossed lips.

His sweet angel, who'd been with him when he'd been dreaming about *Playboy* bunnies, and when he'd ended up tossing his cookies at her feet.

Oh, yeah, *that* had been a highlight.

Still the sight of her made him want to smile. When he did, a whole new kind of pain swam through him. "Oh, shit."

"Careful." She cupped his jaw, her hand blessedly cool on his burning skin. "Stay still."

He let out a raw laugh. "Yeah. Not so good at that."

"I'd suggest trying."

She'd seen him at his absolute worst and was still here. Other than Hawk, that was a rarity for him. And worth everything. He could look at her all day. Hell, all week. He felt dazzled. Dizzy.

But that might have been the pain meds. "You stayed."

She put her deliciously cool hand on his forehead. "I'm glad you're back."

"When was I gone?"

"You've been pretty out of it. Your boss called and he sounded devastated at what had happened to you."

"Tibbs?"

"I didn't catch his name. He said he'd see you soon."

"Southern accent so thick he sounds like his cheeks are filled with marbles?"

"No. Sort of a rushed, clipped voice."

At that, images flashed to him from the barn. Everything going to shit. The shadow on the roof with him. Looking down and seeing something, someone on the ground, looking up at him just before the hit to the head.

Gaines.

He knew that now. He'd looked into Gaines's eyes and yet had been hit from behind.

By one of Gaines's men. *Bastard.*

"You were out for a long time."

That sounded bad. He only vaguely remembered being loaded from the chopper into the hospital, but he definitely remembered this gorgeous angel hovering over him with those sweet eyes and that mouth that made him think of hot, sweaty sex. He tried to lift a hand to touch her and found it taped to a board with two separate IVs hooked up to his arm. Uh-oh. Locating his other hand, he slapped at his legs to make sure they were both still there, and a searing bolt of pain sang up his right leg. This time he couldn't even swear, much less breathe.

"Oh, Logan, don't." She ran a hand down his arm in a slow, comforting manner. "Just hang tight. And don't move."

He gasped for breath. "Just—give it to me straight. My injuries."

She looked him right in the eyes. "Well, you have some."

"Some? Or so many they can't be counted?"

Her lips quirked. Her eyes softened. "Somewhere in the middle."

A sense of humor. With eyes like that and a mouth made for sin, it was sensory overload. "Tell me."

"Let me get your doctor—"

Somehow he managed to grab her hand and hold her still. "I want to hear it from you."

"Well, you have quite a concussion."

"Okay, that explains why my head feels like it was stitched back onto my neck."

"Yep, eighteen stitches."

"Ouch."

"There was some concern about the length of time you were unconscious, but you're awake now, and that's all the matters." She stroked her fingers over his. "Right?"

He stared at her fingers. Long, strong, capable. Ringless. "Absolutely. Awake is good, but...? I thought I heard a big one at the end of that statement."

"Logan."

Oh, yeah. His humor faded. "Spill it."

"You fractured your right leg and three ribs in the fall."

"I've had worse." Which was true.

"There's some internal bleeding that's causing concern. They were worried one of your ribs might have punctured a lung—"

"Hey, I'm breathing just fine."

She nodded and smoothed his blanket, looking so touchingly concerned he wanted to pull her into his lap and kiss it away. Too bad he hurt so much that he was in danger of puking again.

She read his expression with alarming accuracy. "Do you need—"

"No." He would not throw up again in front of her if it was the last thing he didn't do.

"Well...I should probably go. I'll get your doctor first—"

"No." Logan tightened his grip on her hand, about to utter two words he'd never said before, to anyone. "Don't go."

"I really shouldn't be here."

"And yet you are."

"But I shouldn't be," she repeated with a helpless smile. "I don't know why. I just..."

"What?"

"Nothing."

"Come on. I puked in front of you. Give me something."

She glanced back at the door. "It sounds so silly, like a cliché, but I felt this...connection..."

"I know." He'd felt it too, and he didn't do connections. Not breaking eye contact, he pulled her closer until she sat on the edge of his bed.

"So you felt it, too?" She asked this casually, just like this wasn't the moment he usually ran like hell from. If he couldn't run, he typically backpedaled, scrambling to make up whatever it was that a woman needed to hear, whatever it took to get her back into bed, or into her clothes and out his door, whatever *he* happened to need at the time.

He could be, as Hawk liked to say, a real prick.

But Logan preferred to think of it like this: it took

little to no effort at all to compliment a woman, to touch her the way she wanted to be touched, to listen when she spoke. They loved it.

And he loved being loved.

Normally, by the time he backed out of whatever budding relationship he had going, moving into different waters, the woman he'd been with felt great about themselves.

Both parties happy.

But staring into his angel's eyes, he suddenly had no fancy words, no moves. He had nothing, and as the silence grew, her smile faded. She stood.

"No, wait. I'm—"

"Sorry? Don't be. It's okay." She shook her head. "It's my fault. I shouldn't have stayed. You just rest now, and—"

"Your name," he said hoarsely. Christ, his chest hurt.

"What?"

She tried to pull free but he didn't let go of her, couldn't, because suddenly, seriously, his chest hurt like hell. And it wasn't from his fall. "I don't even know your name."

"I've got to go." Gently but firmly she broke loose and turned to the door, and Logan closed his eyes. The irony didn't escape him. When it came to women, he did the leaving, he always had. A shrink would have a field day with the reasons for his behavior, but he didn't care about any of that now, except that for the first time in his life, the roles were reversed.

She was leaving him.

It didn't matter that he'd known her for all of a

handful of minutes. That he didn't even know her fucking name. That he was injured, and he had no idea where or how Hawk was, or how the take-down had turned out.

Nothing mattered but this, crazy as it was. "Please, wait."

Hand on the door, she went still but didn't look at him.

More pain in his chest. Ah, now he got it. Not his chest, but his heart. He stared at her slim spine, at the lush red hair that he wanted to bury his face in. *Turn around*, he silently willed.

She didn't. Of course she didn't.

Because for once, he wasn't in charge, and he had no choice but to reveal himself. "I felt it.".

Pivoting around, she locked her eyes on his. "What?"

"The connection. If you meant this thing zinging between us at the approximate speed of sound, possibly even the speed of light, then, yeah." He cleared his throat, and did something utterly new.

Bared his soul. "I *felt* it."

She looked down at her feet, then back into his eyes. "Callen. My name is Callen O'Malley."

"Well, Callen O'Malley…" He held out his hand. "Now that I've puked in front of you, not to mention been delirious and probably an all around class A asshole to boot, maybe I could show you a different side of me. A better side."

She arched an eyebrow. "And what side would that be? I've already seen every inch."

One glance at the hospital gown he wore instead of his ATF gear was all the explanation of that statement he needed. "I hope they were the good inches."

She smiled, and he felt like he'd won the jackpot. And when she stepped back toward him, he thought he could just die right now, because for the first time in hours, hell years, he felt like everything was going to be okay.

"You going to tell me the plan?"

Hawk glanced at Abby in surprise. She hadn't spoken to him in thirty-three minutes. He knew because he was still holding her phone and he'd glanced at the readout at least a thousand times.

By some miracle, they hadn't been followed, but they were on borrowed time. He had only until their pursuers caught up to them to figure out a concrete plan for getting Abby somewhere safe, and then to her computer. "She speaks."

"Hostages don't speak. We suffer."

He glanced over at her, but she was already shaking her head. "Forget I said that."

Yeah, okay. Except he never forgot a thing. Not how she'd gone running out into the night from the relative safety of the van into the woods because she'd been worried about him, or how she'd sounded when she'd found him slumped on the ground. Or the feel of her arching against him as he'd kissed her.

At the time he hadn't been sure if she'd meant to pull him closer or push him away, but he knew better now. She'd meant to shoot him.

Only she hadn't.

"I need to make a stop," she said.

"Hungry?"

"No."

"Thirsty?"

She shifted in her seat, looking uncomfortable. "No."

"Then no stop."

"I have to go to the bathroom."

Damn it. The one excuse he had no defense against. Pulling off the highway at the next exit, he drove into the only thing around, a campground with a sign that read Lost Hills. The sign didn't lie, the place was rugged, remote. Indeed, someone could easily get lost here. The guard station was empty, and Hawk chose to take that as the first good sign in an otherwise entirely shitty evening.

Maybe his luck was changing.

He drove down the bumpy one-lane road, eyeing all the campsites, which were empty. Normal people didn't camp in northern Wyoming in the late fall, because it would freeze your body parts off cold. The road had plenty of turnoffs, and he picked an out-of-the-way spot. Pleased, he turned to Abby.

Who was distinctly not pleased. "I don't see a bathroom," she said.

"Well—"

"And don't you dare point to a tree."

Which was exactly what he'd been about to do. "I'll close my eyes."

"How do you know that I won't gut you when you do?"

He sighed, the exhaustion creeping up on him like a sledgehammer to the side of the head. "Because you're not crazy about blood."

She let out a disbelieving laugh.

"Look, kill me if you have to, I'm feeling halfway dead anyway." He scrubbed a hand over his face. "And if you don't, we'll take off again when you're ready.

"To go to my place for my computer, and then we flush out Gaines. Right?"

There was going to be an "and then." His head swam for a moment, probably from sheer exhaustion. That, and an odd need to ask her to repeat the "we."

There hadn't been many "we's" in his life. Not once a woman realized his long hours and dangerous work would keep him just a little too gone, and way too distant. Few had hung in there, seeing past the job to the man beneath.

"Right. We'll stick to the plan." Well, mostly. Except for the part where she was with him when he flushed out Gaines.

"And if the numbers don't match…?" she pressed.

It was a good question. A fair question. "The numbers will match."

"Right. And you know this because your instincts tell you so." Abby laughed, completely mirthlessly, and covered her eyes, leaning her head back against the headrest.

"You never explained. What's your attachment to Gaines, anyway?"

She shot him a look that said *none of your business*. Well that, and *go to hell*. Preferably yesterday.

"Look," he told her. "I can promise you, I am not the bad guy here." Hawk felt that bore repeating. Over and over. But when he took in her ashen face and the bruises forming around her wrist, he grimaced. "Okay, I didn't *mean* to be the bad guy."

She turned away and made him feel like shit. "Abby, please. Look at me."

After a hesitation, she leveled him with those wide baby blues.

"I woke up this morning and I *was* the good guy. I was on the verge of bringing down the Kiddie Bombers. Then I went to the raid and ended up fighting off our boss."

"It's just all so hard to swallow—"

He thrust her cell at her. "Call him. I guarantee you, you're never going to hear from him again."

Taking the phone, she flipped it open and stared down at the keypad. "What am I supposed to say? Excuse me, but are you the bad guy? Because Hawk says you are."

"And because you know it, too."

Her eyes met his for one long beat.

"Call," he whispered.

She hit a number and he realized she had Elliot on her speed dial, which gave him a ridiculous twist in the gut as the green-eyed monster took over for a moment.

"Elliot," she said softly, her gaze locked on Hawk's. "Can you call me?" Slowly Abby shut the phone, staring down at it as if she expected it to vibrate any second.

"So," he said, much lighter than he felt. "How long ago did the two of you…?" He waggled an eyebrow.

She sighed. "I'm not doing the boss, Hawk."

"You've dated."

"A few times," she agreed. "A very long time ago. A lifetime ago." She gazed out the window into the dark night, looking so sad it made him hurt.

"Look, obviously I'm missing a big piece of this puzzle. If we're going to figure this all out, I should know everything." Bullshit. He wanted to know for other reasons. Personal reasons. "Talk to me, Ab."

Letting out an uneven breath, she dipped her head down so that she was staring at her lap. "We need to sleep."

"Soon. Talk to me."

"Do you remember the Seattle raid last year that went bad?"

He remembered because it was the first time in several years that an agent had been injured on the job. A female agent, if he remembered correctly, who'd been caught and held captive, tortured for information—

Ah, Christ. "No—"

"It was me." She slanted him a quick glance to make sure she had his attention. As if he could do anything but look at her, sick to his very soul. "Gaines rescued me."

Stunned, he just sat there. She was telling the truth, at least as she knew it. No one could fake that look on her face, or the tinge of hero worship that the rescue had no doubt created. *Shit*, he thought, realizing how much he was asking of her to believe Gaines had done all he'd done.

"I didn't know," he said very quietly, staring at the raw skin on her wrist. In all likelihood it was nothing compared to what she'd suffered last year.

"Afterward, I took some time off," she whispered. "Gaines encouraged that. And then when I was ready to get back to work, he put me here because I could be in communications, out of the action."

"I'm surprised you came back to work at all."

"I know. Me, too. But I didn't want to let them take this from me. I had to prove something to myself."

And he'd put her right back into the nightmare. Knowing it, he hated himself. "Abby—"

"Funny thing is, I felt safe, too." She closed her eyes. "Until I left the van."

He wanted to kick his own ass. "Abby, God. I'm so sorry—"

"Don't." She shook her head, still very carefully not looking at him. "Don't be sorry. I'm fine."

She didn't want his pity. He wouldn't have wanted any either. But that didn't change the basic facts. She'd overcome one nightmare, and now was living a new one.

"I need to talk to Logan," he said. "And to Watkins and Thomas. To see exactly what we're up against."

She said nothing but fed him a long stare. *Right*. She didn't do "we," she didn't do trust either, at least not for him. "We're in this now, for better or worse."

"Through sickness and health?" Her eyes flashed in brief good humor. "Just don't even think about asking me to obey. Or to sleep in this truck with you."

If nothing else, he had to admire her sheer will and the inner strength he'd only suspected existed before. He couldn't imagine all she'd gone through—or maybe the problem was he *could*, in great detail, and it made him want to personally hunt down each and every single one of her demons and kill them for her. "No, we're not going to sleep in the truck. I have a friend with a B&B. We can grab some shut-eye there, and get to your place in the morning, okay?"

Abby stared at him so long he figured the gig was up, she was done with him. But finally she nodded. She wasn't over her mistrust of him, not yet, but neither was she still fighting him. And after the night he'd had, he felt grateful for the small favor. But first…

Hawk gestured to the nearest grove of trees with his hand. "Would you like me to escort you to the facilities?"

11

ABBY JERKED AWAKE. Sitting straight up, heart in her throat, she nearly leaped right out of her skin when Hawk set a hand on her arm.

"Easy," he said softly. "Just me."

She'd been deeply asleep, dreamless, which was a miracle in its own right, but that she'd actually for a moment forgotten where she was and who she was with and what they were doing...

The truck was parked and turned off. That's probably what had woken her. It was still dark but with the very hint of a lightening of the sky in the far east. Almost dawn. She probably looked like a disaster.

Hawk stroked a finger over her temple, pushing a strand of hair off her face. "You all the way awake?" he asked.

"Yeah." The dash clash read 5:05 a.m. "What I can't believe is that I slept." She pulled free of his touch and scrubbed a hand over her face. "Given our situation."

"Remember, we're the good guys. We've done nothing wrong."

"Except flee the crime scene."

"The crime scene in which we were the victims."

"It's still not okay that we just left—"

"It was that or die," he said flatly, and she took a good long look at him. His eyes were shadowed and so was his jaw. There was a weariness to the way he sat in the driver's seat that told her he was still hurting, still exhausted, and on the very edge.

"We're only forty-five minutes out of Cheyenne." He jutted his chin toward the outside of the truck, for the first time drawing her gaze to where he'd stopped.

They were on a long, wide street lined by huge oak trees, wooden sidewalks and old-fashioned cabin-style houses all clean and neat and exuding charm and personality. It looked like the wild, wild West all cleaned up. "Where are we?"

"B&B row, Old West style. They've done up this town like it was back then—for the tourists. I need to get a few hours sleep, Abby, or I'm going to do something stupid."

She slid him a long look. "Like?"

"Like…" He slid his thumb over her jaw, his gaze filled with things that made her swallow hard.

And there were other reactions as well, reactions that reminded her that he was a man, an exceedingly sensual, sexy, hot man, and that she was all woman.

Yowza. She'd nearly forgotten what lust felt like. "If we could just get to my computer—"

Hawk was shaking his head before she even finished her sentence.

"If you're too tired to keep driving," she said. "I'll do it."

"I don't think so."

Disbelief filled her. "Let me get this straight. I'm supposed to trust you, but you don't have to trust me?" She couldn't help but sound a little bitter at this one. "That's ridiculous! I'm the innocent one here. I'm the one to be trusted!"

"Because you promised to make this as difficult and painful as possible, remember?"

Okay, he had her there.

"And you haven't yet decided to finally trust me."

And there.

"What do you think I'm going to do, anyway?" she asked.

He laughed and rubbed a weary hand over his face. "Oh, I don't know. Turn me in to Tibbs before I can prove my innocence." He shrugged out of his flak vest and outer shirt, leaving him in just the black T-shirt. "I'm sorry, but I'm not going to go to sleep only to wake up to you driving me directly to the ATF. I left my Get Out of Jail Free card at home."

"If we just went to Regional and laid out all the events in the order that they happened, I'm sure—"

"Sure what? That I'll get a fair trial before death row?"

"If you're innocent—"

"If? Jesus, Abby." Sending her a stare that was filled with just enough hurt to stab right at her heart, he got out of the truck and slammed the door.

Abby shook her head at herself. Truth was, she

believed him. Or she wanted to. How terrifying was that? With a sigh, she followed, the pre-dawn air slapping her face, stinging her skin. "Hawk, wait."

He tipped his head up at the still-dark sky, then turned to look at her, his expression pure resistance, frustration—and also reluctant affection.

God.

It was that, that got her. Because a murderer would not be looking at her as if he couldn't decide between kissing her and wrapping his fingers around her neck, would he?

"I didn't mean…" She trailed off, and he looked as if he was resisting the urge to thunk his head on the trunk of the truck.

Straightening, he drew in a deep breath and lifted his hands, stabbing them into his hair. The muscles in his shoulders and arms were tense, straining the sleeves of his T-shirt.

She'd experienced his strength firsthand last night and did not want to go another round with him.

Which did not in any way explain the little quiver that occurred low in her belly.

"I called about Logan while you were asleep," he said. "He's still in intensive care." Hawk shook his head. "He didn't fall from that roof. No way in hell." He dropped his arms to his side and let her see everything he was feeling, which was more of that rage, frustration, exhaustion and also an underlying need for her to believe in him. "He didn't call you back."

Yeah. She'd noticed. If Gaines was on the up and up, and alive, he'd have called her back. Unless, of course, he really was dead. "Maybe the fire did get him—"

"It didn't."

"How do you know he didn't die from his gunshot?"

"It was a flesh wound. Nothing more. And now he has the ultimate freedom."

Abby shut her door and came around to the front of the truck to face him. "You're certain he's not dead."

Fingers still shoved in his hair, he closed his eyes and drew a breath. "I'd stake my life on it."

His body was taut as an arrow. She came up only to his shoulders, and she knew damn well he could have used physical force to coerce her to do whatever he wanted, but other than when she'd lost it completely last night, he hadn't. In fact, he'd done everything within his power not to hurt her, even when she'd hurt him.

Then he opened his eyes and let her look at him, into him, hiding nothing at all. She peered into his face for a long beat and he stared straight back at her, as if he was hoping to hell she was finding the honesty she sought because he couldn't possibly lay himself more bare.

"The Gaines I know loves justice," she finally said.

"No, he loves to win."

Yes, that was true, too. He'd taken great pride in all the cases he'd closed, and that was no secret.

"I realize you have a bond with him." Hawk said this just a little too tightly, as if maybe he hated thinking about it.

"He saved me," she reminded him.

He shocked her by reaching for her hand. "I know."

She stared down at their joined fingers. "Hawk?"

"Yeah?"

"Just before I was taken, I'd been working on the Kiddie Bombers."

"Yeah? There were a lot of agents across the whole western region doing so."

"I felt like I was really making a breakthrough." Her voice trailed off and they stared at each other. "This is insane," she whispered. "You know that."

"Insane, but real."

"He saved me from the very men that you'd like to prove work for him. My God. He did this, he set all this up."

He squeezed her fingers. "Yeah. I think so. Abby, I'm sorry, but I will prove it."

Her gaze searched his. "He knew who had me. He let them have me." Images bombarded her, the terror, the overwhelming certainty that she was dead. And then being all too alive— "He ordered me held captive," she repeated in disbelief.

"God, Abby." His low, husky voice brought her back. "I don't want to dredge it up for you, I just—"

"You just want me to know that the reason I made it out of there alive is the only reason that I was there in the first place." Sickened, she closed her eyes.

"I think he wanted to make himself the good guy. Your good guy."

The men who'd taken her had been well-versed in how to get the answers they wanted. And what

they'd wanted from her was any concrete knowledge she had on the Kiddie Bombers, which hadn't
been all that much. But she'd been chained up, then
left alone in the pitch-black for four long hours
before they'd come for her, knowing by then she'd
be half out of her mind. And she had been.

They'd just begun to really have fun with her
while she'd been trying desperately to pretend she
was somewhere, anywhere, else, when Gaines had
come in, gun drawn, taking two of her assailants out
without blinking.

The other two had run like scared little bunnies
while Gaines had freed her and carried her out.

She'd never questioned how he'd known, how he'd
killed only two of the four and yet been able to get
her out of there without either of them being killed.

It had never occurred to her to be anything but
grateful. *Extremely* grateful.

"Abby."

She opened her eyes.

Hawk had stepped close. "I hate bringing you
back there." He slid his hands in her hair. "I hate myself for making you think about it at all. But my life
depends on it.

"I can't think this way," she whispered. "I'll fall
apart."

"Then *I'll* think that way. All I'm asking you to do
is give me a chance. Don't send me to the gallows yet."

"So what now? Do you think we're going to go
in there and I'm going to sleep with you?"

"No, I think *I'm* going to sleep, and you're possibly going to stab me in my sleep. Which is slightly preferable to going to jail."

"Okay," she said softly.

"Okay, what? You're going to stab me in my sleep?"

"I guess you'll have to take your chances on that, won't you." She turned and headed up the front walk to the door. Her clothes felt damp and icy, though she knew that was more from shock than anything else because Hawk had been running the heater in the truck for hours.

But she felt as if she'd never get warm again.

He caught up with her with his long-legged stride, and reached out and took her hand in a sweet gesture.

Or maybe to keep her from running. Although where he thought she was going to run off to, she had no idea.

Opening the rough wooden gate, he let her in. There were several low lights lining the walk, illuminating an antique-covered wagon in the front yard and the house, complete with old-style shutters and white lace curtains hanging in the windows. The yard itself was thick with growth. She took her first deep breath in hours, and smelled fresh-cut grass and the scent of myriad different blooms.

Behind her, the gate clicked closed and she knew Hawk was right on her heels. Watching her closely. Was he looking at her wild hair? Her grubby clothes? She glanced back—

Um. Yes. He was noticing all the above, and more. When his gaze lifted and met hers, he didn't try to be coy or reserved, or anything other than who he was, and he had no problem letting her see him.

All of him.

Everything he felt, which pretty much ran the gamut. Oh, God. She'd never been so aware of another human being in all her life, standing so close she could feel his soft exhale on her temple, could see deep into his warm eyes. He was just so…overwhelmingly male. Did he know the confusion he aroused? Or that when he stared at her like that she had certain reactions she couldn't seem to help? She crossed her arms over her chest, because, seriously, she had a problem. How could her body react in this manner, when with the other side of her brain she was recoiling in horror at the evening's events? "This is crazy," she whispered. "I don't want to look at you and—"

"And what?"

"Hawk."

"And what, Ab? Want me?"

"I don't…want you." Trying to be casual, she dropped her arms to her side.

His gaze fell to the front of her shirt, which revealed her traitorous nipples, hard and pressing against the fabric of her shirt. She felt the heat rush to her cheeks. He should have at least pretended not to notice.

Instead his eyes blazed with a new awareness, and a staggering heat that almost equalled the explosions they'd faced earlier.

Oh, God. Was this really happening?

"Abby—"

But whatever he'd planned on saying was lost as

the front door opened. There in the doorway stood a stunningly beautiful brunette in a cream silk bathrobe that hugged her spectacular curves. Her smile came slow and sure as she took in the sight of Hawk on her doorstep. "Well, look what the cat dragged in."

He smiled back. "Serena."

Serena tossed back her long, thick hair and crossed her arms, which as she undoubtedly knew, plumped up her substantial breasts from a D-plus to at least a triple-F. "My my. I guess hell froze over?"

"If you only knew." Hawk's smile remained easy and charming, and completely confident in the manner of a man who always got his own way. "Do you have a room available?"

"*Two* rooms," Abby clarified.

"One," Hawk repeated.

"Two, or nothing," Abby said through her teeth.

Hawk sighed. "Connecting. We'll take connecting rooms."

Serena divided a glance between them, then tossed back her head and laughed. "Oh, boy, Hawk. I think you've finally met your match."

12

STANDING IN THE pre-dawn chill, Abby craned her neck and stared at Hawk. She'd thought tonight couldn't get any more Twilight Zone–like. "Your match?"

"Serena has a very peculiar sense of humor." He shot Serena a long look. "Any second now she's going to let us in off her doorstep and put us in a room, and then go far, far away."

Serena smiled but didn't budge. "Oh, but this is so much more fun. So." She turned to Abby. "You been dating him long?"

Abby opened her mouth to correct that impression, but Serena went on. "No, it can't have been too long, because, after all, you're still with him." She grinned at herself. "That means you haven't discovered his character flaws yet."

Next to Abby, Hawk let out a sigh.

Abby shook her head at Serena. "You've gotten the wrong idea—"

"Oh, believe me, honey. I know how hard it is to give him up."

Abby doubted that greatly. Hawk was a handful, not to mention most likely walking/talking heartbreak. She could give him up just like that.

Probably.

"It's a little like walking away from double-fudge chocolate cake, isn't it?" Serena asked. "Harder than anything, but in the end, you save yourself the bellyache."

"I'm not all that fond of chocolate cake in the first place," Abby replied.

Serena let out a deep laugh. "You know what? I like you already." She elbowed Abby. "At least the sex is off the charts amazing, right?"

"Can we focus?" Hawk asked, sounding pained.

Off the charts? Abby had little reference for "off the charts amazing." She didn't want to know, she reminded herself. Okay, mostly didn't want to know….

Ah, hell. She wanted to know.

"If we could just get a room," Hawk said.

"Two," Abby corrected. "*Two* rooms." No off the charts sex today, thank you very much.

Serena looked at Hawk, and at whatever she saw in his face, maybe it was the grim set of his jaw, or, gee, maybe the cut over his eye, she nodded, stepped back and gestured them into the inn.

The main room was large and had a fire going, which Abby headed directly toward. Serena held Hawk back. "Sorry about the heckling," she said softly. "I couldn't seem to help myself."

"Forget it."

"Are you all right?"

"I will be."

Abby turned back to see her touch Hawk's cheek,

her smile now tinged with fondness and some lingering heat. "Anything you need?"

"In spite of my character flaws?" he asked her drily, but he patted her hand with his.

Serena smiled and hugged him, the gesture warm and familiar, the affection unmistakable. "Food?" she asked.

"Sleep."

She nodded. "And a change of clothes."

"That would be—"

"Off the charts amazing?" Serena let out a low laugh. "Sorry about that, couldn't resist."

And Hawk blushed.

Blushed.

Huh. If Abby had set her sights on Hawk, which she so hadn't, she might have been flooded with jealousy at the obvious ease and warmth between them. As it was, she felt nothing.

Liar, liar pants on fire...

She concentrated on the pretty room. The hardwood floors were scarred and covered in throw rugs, the furniture was well used but large and very comfortable looking. Butter-colored walls carried old-fashioned black-and-white pictures from the Wild West. She stuck her hands out to the flames, listening to Hawk and Serena murmur to each other behind her. After a moment, he settled a hand on her shoulder, gesturing for her to come with him, and they headed out of the large room behind Serena, whose hips sashayed beneath that silky robe.

She obviously wasn't wearing anything beneath it.

Abby glanced at Hawk, sure he'd be staring at that lush body, but he was looking right at her. "You okay?" he murmured.

She nodded. She was okay. Maybe even more okay than she'd imagined.

Serena led them upstairs, down a hallway to the last door on the right, which she opened. Hawk nudged Abby in, and though she was drawn to the small but quaint bedroom with its huge rustic wood bed piled high in fluffy bedding, she immediately turned back. "This is one room."

"And a bathroom." Serena pointed to a door.

"But—"

Serena looked at Hawk, then back to Abby. "It's the only room available, hon, sorry."

She was lying. For Hawk's sake. Abby looked at his shirt. Most of the blood had been on the outer shirt, which he'd left in the truck, but there were still some dubious dark stains on his black ATF T-shirt as well.

Why wasn't she telling Serena she needed to use the phone, that she needed help?

Because there was a voice deep inside that said Hawk could be right. That Gaines was lethal, deadly, dangerous. *That* thought made it hard for her to breathe so she did her damnedest not to think at all.

After a minute, Serena left them alone, and when Hawk shut the door, silence reverberated around them nearly as loud as one of the explosions they'd lived through last night.

One room.

One bed.

One really beautiful, lush-looking bed that in no time at all was going to be holding a tall, leanly muscled man who drew her like no one else ever had.

But she didn't want to be drawn.

He let out a low laugh and kicked off his shoes. "You're thinking pretty loudly."

"Sorry."

"Don't be. But let's just say I can tell you're still half convinced you need to call the cops on me."

Not half, but certainly an eighth… "So who's Serena, a girlfriend?"

"An old friend."

"She didn't touch you like a friend."

That brought a ghost of a smile. She realized now that he'd put on that carefree, easygoing air for Serena, because he was not in a joking, light-hearted mood at all. "Jealous?"

"Ha," she said, without any real rancor behind it. Just when she thought she had him all figured out, he revealed another side.

Who the hell was he?

Proving he had more layers than an onion, Hawk pulled out her cell and checked on Logan's status again, clearly concerned. "I need to talk to him," he said to someone on the phone, then paused and frowned. "Yes, I realize he's gravely injured, but—" Listening, he pinched the bridge of his nose. "Okay, thank you." He disconnected. "Damn it. No change."

"But he's alive," she reminded him.

"True enough." He punched in a different number.

"What are you doing?"

"Calling his cell."

"But he won't—"

"No, but someone else might."

"Like who?"

"Like whoever is at his side—hello," Hawk said into the phone, looking surprised. "Who's this? Logan's nurse? Perfect. This is Conner Hawk, his partner, and—oh." He paused. "You know about me—he was awake?" He nodded. "Yeah, we're family. How is he?" After a few seconds, he visibly relaxed. "You've just made my day, Callen—no, I understand the severity of his injuries but, see, he's going to recover. Yeah, trust me, best news I've had in hours. Can I talk to him? It's urgent—" He listened intently. "Yeah, I heard him. Tell him to watch his six. It's in danger, too." He paused again. "Right. And no visitors. None, not even a high-ranking ATF official, can you manage that? Yeah, I'm serious. This is serious. As serious as it gets."

"Hawk. A nurse won't stop Gaines."

"Callen," Hawk said without missing a beat. "I need to get him moved. What are the chances of that?" He stalked the length of the room, his long legs churning up the space in two strides before he had to spin to walk again. "Yeah. It's life or death. Logan's life or death—yes, that would do it. Switch his chart, change his name. Disguise him, if you have to. Hell, put him where he won't be expected. No, definitely away from the ER—" He smiled. "Yeah. That'll work."

"Where?" Abby asked.

Hawk grinned. "Maternity," he whispered to her. "Callen? He's going to fight this. Tell him too fucking bad." He listened again, then nodded. "Okay. And tell him—" He stopped smiling. "Tell him to get his sorry ass healed, that's his job now. That I'll be there in a few hours. And thanks. I owe you more than you'll ever know." He shut the phone, then stood there for a long moment.

"Hawk?"

He looked at her. "He's bad off."

Shocked at an urge to wrap her arms around him, she hugged herself instead. "I know. I'm sorry."

"But still, he made sure I got the message."

"Message?"

"Someone called, said he was Logan's boss. Asked about his status."

"Tibbs."

"No southern accent."

As she processed that, he went on. "And then Tibbs did call, complete with accent. To tell him that they found a body at the barn. Unidentifiable, because it's burned beyond recognition. It's still crazy up there, the fire is uncontrolled, but they're presuming it's Gaines. Do you want the first shower?"

"No, we need my laptop, Hawk. We should go now." It would give her one answer at least, and she needed that.

"We'll get there." He began tossing the contents of his pockets to the nightstand—her cell phone… the handcuffs. He pulled off his shirt, which left him standing there in dangerously low-slung jeans and a pair of socks, which he toed off.

"W-what are you doing?"

"Stripping," he said as if that was the most natural thing in the world to be doing.

"Yes, but—"

Every breath he took seemed to threaten the decency level of his waistband. There was a gap between the denim and the most amazing six-pack abs she'd ever seen. In another time and place there was no way she could have resisted shoving her hand down that gap to go treasure hunting.

Well, except for one thing.

She'd never been that bold a day in her life.

He reached for the buttons on the Levi's. "I'm going to shower. Tell me I don't need to worry while I'm in there."

Pop went the first button on his jeans.

Pop went the second button.

Oh, God. He'd revealed a wedge of skin that was paler than the skin covering his chest and belly. "Um—"

Eyes serious but warm, he mercifully stopped the unbuttoning. "Look, I just want a shower and some shut-eye. I can sleep on the floor, you can have the bed, I don't care. I just have to recharge for a few hours, that's all. Tell me you're not going to steal the truck, Ab."

"You mean the truck that *you* stole first—"

Hawk acknowledged that with a slight nod of his

head. "I just need to know you and that truck are going to be here when I get out."

"Because you need my computer."

"Because I don't need to come out to be surrounded by the cops."

Pop.

She couldn't help it. Maybe once she'd been brave, but all that courage had left her, and she covered her eyes.

"Abby?" She felt him shift closer, and then his big, callused palms slid up and down her limbs in a gesture that was somehow soothing, yet made her want to leap right out of her skin. "Hey," he whispered. "Don't give up on me now." Up and down. Down and up.

The cold she'd felt only minutes ago had deserted her entirely. *What was the matter with her?* She opened her eyes and found her vision filled with his torso, the light from the lamp behind him blocked out by his broad shoulders. She had no idea what it was about a naked male chest that spun her wheels, had no idea such a shallow thing even could, but there it was. Lust, pure and simple, buzzed through her system and made her punch drunk.

"We're so close," he murmured, apparently clueless to what his hands were doing to her.

Yes. Yes, she was. Close to orgasmic bliss.

"After a quick catnap, we get your laptop," he said. "And then we draw out Gaines."

She dropped her gaze. Took in the scar over one

pec. Without thinking, she ran a finger over it, eliciting a low sound from him.

"Abby." His voice was hoarse. "What are you doing?"

She had no idea. "Just standing here." She jerked her hand away from him.

"You were touching me. Looking at me. Like you wanted a bite of me."

"No." *Yes.*

Backing away, he lifted his hands in the air, then turned from her, once again shoving his fingers in his short hair. His unbuttoned jeans had slid down, revealing a line of black cotton and a sleek spine that was as edible as the rest of him.

Hawk headed to the bathroom, popping open that last button as he went. "Just…say you're going to be here when I get out."

Eyes glued to the seat of his jeans, which had slid to an almost indecent level, she couldn't quite have answered the age-old question of briefs or boxers, but any second now—

"Abby?"

Her gaze jerked up as he turned. Oh, God. And caught her staring. Eyes narrowed, he lifted a hand and pointed a finger at her. "That." He sounded more than a little off his axis. "What the hell was *that?*"

"N-nothing."

Walking back toward her, he let out a sound of disbelief. "No, that wasn't nothing. That was…heat. That was lust."

She covered her face. "I'm sorry."

A low laugh escaped him. "Abigail Wells, were you just lusting after me?"

"No." She winced. "A little, maybe."

He stared at her for one long beat. "Maybe or most definitely?"

Again she bit her lip.

"Look, you were just looking at me as if I was a twelve-course meal and you'd been fasting for two days. That, or you're plotting my slow, painful murder."

"A little of both, I think."

"Okay, I really need to go now."

"Hawk—"

But she was talking to his back. And as he walked into the bathroom, he kicked his Levi's to the floor.

Knit boxers.

Then the door shut, leaving her standing there, knees a little bit wobbly. Her kidnapper had just flashed her the best buns she'd ever seen.

HAWK CAME OUT OF THE SHOWER with some trepidation. He'd faced war, he'd faced gangs, he'd faced a whole hell of a lot just in the past twenty-four hours alone, but now his stomach actually hurt as he opened the bathroom door and waited for the steam to dissipate, because this time he had no idea what was waiting for him.

Utter silence and pitch blackness.

Clearly Abby had shut the shades, but he couldn't even hear her breathing, and he had some damn fine hearing.

Not. Good. "Abby?"

Nothing.

Christ. She was probably halfway to Cheyenne by now, with the police on their way here to take him to jail for a whole host of crimes he hadn't committed.

He'd trusted her. He'd trusted her and she'd stabbed him in the damn heart. God, he really was an ass. Pissed, and more hurt than he cared to acknowledge, Hawk stepped into the dark room and tripped over the bed, then nearly had heart failure when someone lurched off the mattress and hit the floor with a small cry.

Abby.

"Oh, God. I'm sorry." Rushing forward, hands out to find her, he felt a soft, curvy form and dropped to his knees at her side.

She was doubled over, hands on her knees, gasping for breath.

"Abby—" Eyes adjusted, he reached out to touch her, but was not surprised when she jerked back with another small cry, an animal sound really, that caused a sharp pain in his chest.

He'd felt pretty damn small several times in the past eight hours but that moment topped them all. It was the way he'd brought her here, of course, against her will. "Abby."

"Don't."

Don't what? Don't touch? Don't look? Don't do any damn thing, likely enough. "You were sleeping."

She didn't answer, just panted as if she'd been running.

"I startled you," he murmured.

"Not you," she said with only a hint of that bravado he loved in her. "*You* didn't scare me."

"Okay." Sitting back on his heels, Hawk studied her outline in the dark. She was still breathing heavily. "You were dreaming. Badly."

She lifted a shoulder. The only admission he was going to get most likely.

"Tibbs called." She said this so quietly that he had to lean in to hear her. When the words soaked into his addled brain, he froze.

Shit. "So should I expect to get my ass hauled out of here any time now?" He asked this with remarkable calm, given that his life was over.

She didn't respond.

"Abby?"

She sighed, and he shook his head. *Perfect.*

13

"ABBY," HAWK SAID AS CALMLY as he could, which wasn't all that calmly. He wondered how much time he had. Ten minutes?

Less?

He should probably get dressed in more than just a damn towel. Because no way did he want to go to prison in only a towel. But before he could move, someone knocked on the door, and pretty much took five years off his life.

In the dark room, Abby drew a deep breath. A sound that held a good amount of guilt.

Damn. He gripped his towel and wished for clean clothes at least. He couldn't even go out the window, they were on the second floor—

Another knock, which didn't help his heart rate any. The way the poor organ had been abused tonight, it was a wonder it was still ticking at all. "Shit," he said again, brilliantly.

"I didn't answer when he called," Abby said quietly.

He stared at her. What did she mean, she hadn't answered the call? Hard to tell in the dark since he couldn't read her expression.

The knock came again. Then Serena's voice. "Hawk?"

Okay, maybe he could get those five years back. Holding onto his towel, he opened the door to find Serena holding a stack of folded clothing. "Hey," she said, and looked him over with frank appreciation before grinning. "Damn." She waggled her eyebrows. "Almost makes me sorry I dumped your workaholic ass."

"Serena—"

"Oh, relax. I know what's good for me and what's not. And you are definitely not." She thrust the clothing at him, which he struggled to grab and also keep a grip on the towel.

Serena appeared to enjoy the battle. "Thought you could use some of the clothes you left here. And I brought Abby something, too. Also, I pulled the truck into my garage."

All irritation at her interruption vanished. "Thanks."

She tried to peer into the dark room behind him, but couldn't. "Also, there's a first aid kit in the pile, for that cut on your head. Do you need a doctor?"

He felt like he'd been hit with a Mack truck, but he was fairly certain he was going to live. "Nah. I'm okay."

"All right, tough guy." Leaning in, she kissed his cheek. "You're in it deep again, aren't you?"

"A little."

"Honey, with you, there's no 'little' anything." And with a smile she walked away.

Hawk shut the door and turned back to the dark room. There she was. Still by the bed.

"Did she love you?"

He couldn't believe that this was the conversation they were going to have before he went to jail. "She used to say she did."

"She still wants you."

He set the clothes on the foot of the bed. "She dumped me."

"Maybe, but that doesn't change her feelings."

Hawk reached for the light.

"Don't, please."

Easing back, he tried to see her. "Abby—"

"You let yourself be loved. I'm just trying to picture this, the big, badass, tough as nails, elusive, edgy Conner Hawk, letting himself be loved by a woman."

"Badass?" With a harsh laugh, he scrubbed a hand over his face. "I don't feel so badass. With you, I feel…"

"What?"

Since she sounded sincerely curious, he decided to tell her. "Like a sorry-ass marshmallow. Am I going to jail, Abby?"

"No."

Relieved, he sank to the mattress. "And why is that?"

"Because while I retrieved Tibbs's message, I didn't speak to him."

"What did he say?"

"That I need to tell him where I am. He said that they found the murder weapon in the clearing near the barn with your prints on the gun. Oh, and the barn was a complete loss—a total burn."

That took some careful planning. Careful planning, and planting of explosives in the right spots.

Knowledge, of course, that Gaines had. "They have my prints because it's my own damn gun," he said tightly. "He took it from me. But how is it that the gun didn't melt in the fire? Pretty damn suspicious if you ask me."

"Agreed."

Hawk didn't know what hit him the hardest—that she'd stayed willingly when given a chance to leave or the quiet word that signaled she was beginning to believe him. It was a good thing he was already sitting, he was that shaky with relief. *God*. He hadn't realized how tense he'd felt, how unnerved, and frankly, how fucking alone.

But he wasn't alone at all. He leaned back against the headboard, and with the same care he'd give a nuclear bomb, reached for her. "Come here."

Shockingly, she let him pull her in. He did so very slowly, not wanting to scare her off, but needing to feel her close. She sat at his side, but went still when he tugged her into the crook of his arm.

"Don't," she choked out.

"Shh. You're okay."

Instead of responding with a slug to the gut as he was more than half braced for, Abby absolutely devastated him by setting her head on his shoulder.

And then she finished him off by turning her face into his neck.

His entire body went still as stone because he was afraid if he moved, hell if he so much as breathed, he'd scare her and she'd scramble away. It shocked him how much he wanted her to stay, just as she was, curled against him, for, oh…the rest of his life.

Holy shit, if that wasn't a thought. His need for her surprised him, but not more so than her clear reflection of it right back at him.

Whether she admitted it or not, she wanted him, too.

She trusted him. An onslaught of tenderness hit him so hard he nearly bawled like a baby. Gently, because he couldn't resist, Hawk pressed his mouth to her temple, brushing his lips across her skin in a light caress, more for comfort than sex, though there were plenty of those urges as well. "You okay?" he whispered.

"I think so. It's the first time I've done this, gotten this physically close since…"

He closed his eyes and struggled not to squeeze her. "I wouldn't do anything to hurt you, Abby. I'd never do anything to hurt you."

"I hurt you." She was quiet a moment. "I hurt you and you didn't hurt me back."

"Yeah. The truth is, you could gut me right here, I'm that helpless when it comes to you. But not you. You are not helpless."

"I was last time."

He drew a careful breath to remain relaxed, as a shocking amount of violence suddenly coursed through him. "I'm sorry. So damned sorry."

"They handcuffed me."

Christ, he wished to God he'd never done that to

her. He wished even more than he could go back in time and be there that day for her.

"To a wall. They took my clothes and brought out these jumper cables, which they said were effective in getting information out of people."

He needed to shoot something. That might help.

"But Gaines rescued me just in time."

He opened his eyes. "Before they—"

"Yes," she whispered. "I was okay."

"Yeah, you are."

"No, I mean I don't hate men or anything…" She let out a little laugh. "Contrary to how I've treated you."

"I can't tell you how very happy I am to hear that you don't hate men, since I'm one. But…"

"But why, if I don't hate men, did I treat you like crap from day one?" she guessed.

Hawk rubbed his jaw over the sweet silk of her hair. "Yeah."

"Apparently not hating men and letting them close are two different ballgames entirely. Up until moving to Cheyenne, it was easy to keep my distance from guys. Probably too easy. Then I met you."

He stopped breathing. "And…?"

"And I couldn't keep my distance. So I pretended."

"Okay, I have to do this." Still moving slowly, he shifted onto his side, pulling her in for a hug, melting a little when she let him.

"You should know…" she said a little shakily "…that contrary to our position, I intend to *keep* my distance."

He ran his jaw over her cheek, loving the softness. "Why?"

"Why?" She let out a little laugh. "Okay, so I'm not sure why exactly."

"You don't have to be afraid of me."

"I'm not."

"And as far as the physical stuff, we could go slow."

"Yeah, see, that I doubt."

Okay, she had a point. Reluctant or not, they had a chemistry, and he imagined if she hadn't been inhibited, they'd already have used at least one condom from the basket on the counter in the bathroom.

"It's been a long time for me, Hawk. A year. If I let us…if we sleep together, I'm not going to be able to take that lightly. And the opposite of not lightly? Not something I'm ready for, and I doubt you are either."

"Ah, Abby." With a sigh, he stroked a hand up her slim spine. "I'm so sorry you were dragged into this."

"I dragged myself in."

He was extremely aware of the fact that she hadn't returned the hug. One of her hands was in her own lap, the other had slipped down and was resting, fist tightly closed, against his abs.

A little higher and she could feel what she'd done to his heart.

A little lower and she'd feel another body part entirely.

But he couldn't help it. He was covered only by the towel, which was pretty insubstantial, and he was holding her.

And she believed him.

Hell, that alone had excited him. But then she let out a shuddery sigh, her breath fanning lightly across his neck in the most incredible sensation he could remember as a strand of her hair stuck to the stubble on his jaw.

He needed to get up, coax her into a shower of her own, and get some sleep, but he didn't want to.

"You can stop worrying about me turning you in," she said, her mouth still against his skin. "I can't do that now. I couldn't live with myself if it turned out everything you've said was true." She lifted her face. "We have to see this through to the end."

Because she humbled him to the core, because he didn't think he could talk through the sudden lump in his throat, he lifted a hand and gently swept back her hair, tucking it behind her ear, using it as an excuse to sink his fingers into her hair while his thumb slid over her cheekbone. "Yeah. We'll see it through. Together." Unable to help himself, he leaned in, but Abby lifted her hand and slapped it to his chest.

"Really, *really* bad idea, remember?"

"I think we're going to have to agree to disagree there, Ab."

"I'm not kidding, Hawk."

Yeah. Damn. He could see that.

"We…" She chewed on her lower lip and stared at his. "We shouldn't."

"So you keep saying. But I gotta tell you, you don't sound all that certain."

"Of course I don't. I'm lying through my teeth."

His heart literally skipped a beat, and unbelievably, he wanted to smile. He wanted to cry and smile at the same time. A true first. Leaning past her, he reached for the lamp.

"No, don't—"

He looked into her eyes. "We've gotten past quite a bit tonight, let's get past this as well, and see each other. I mean really see each other. Okay?"

He could feel her thinking it over. Hell, she was thinking so hard the air shimmered with it, and he brushed his mouth past her cheek. "Come on, Abby. You've trusted me this far…."

"Yeah, well, there's trust, and then there's trust."

"What's the worst that could happen?"

She fell silent, then let out a small laugh that had more nervousness than humor. "I don't know."

"Never fear the unknown." And he flicked on the light.

14

As HAWK TURNED ON THE LIGHT, a warm glow bathed the room. The bed was tousled, and so was the woman in his arms.

"You're naked," she accused him.

"I'm wearing a towel."

"Nearly naked, then." Her breathing had changed, and she wasn't meeting his eyes. But that's because she was soaking him in, from his shoulders to his pecs to his belly, which she seemed to linger over, making the muscles there quiver like…well, like he was a horny teenager about to get lucky for the first time. He felt lucky, so goddamned lucky, even knowing he was crazy to be here, like this, with her.

Insane, he thought, even as his hands fisted in her shirt. Reckless, after what had happened tonight. But she did something to him, to his gut, his heart.

She'd spent six months being cool and icy, shooting him down with her superior disdain. Now he was suddenly beneath that tough veneer, and while he was here, he wanted to ruffle her up, see the real her. He should be running, yet instead he kissed her.

Pulling back, her gaze dipped down his body

again, taking in the towel loosely wrapped around his hips and what it covered.

And what it didn't cover.

But there was the problem. The longer she looked, the less that it covered. Hawk didn't want to freak her out or anything but if she kept it up, which she appeared to be set to do, he wasn't sure that the entire bedspread could cover him. He needed to slow them down, somehow, and opened his mouth to say so, but her tongue came out and wet her lower lip, and he went harder. Great. Nice way to slow down. "Uh, Abby?"

"You're so beautiful," she whispered.

"Not like you. You take my breath." And now the Neanderthal in him wanted to strip her down and get to even more beautiful parts. He wanted it so badly he was shaking, but that was for him. For her...he didn't know what the right thing was, but he wasn't going to rush her, or make the first move. Nope, he was going to sit here and let her look her fill, completely still, nonthreatening, for as long as she wanted.

And if he keeled over from having all his blood between his legs, well then, he hoped she knew CPR. "The last thing I want to do is bring up bad memories."

"No." She shook her head. "I'm okay. I just forgot what it felt like, this...rush."

Okay, looking at him was giving her a rush. He liked that. He liked that a lot. In fact, knowing it gave him a rush of his own.

A big one. One she couldn't possibly miss. But she kept looking, and he kept letting her, for as long as he could, until it had to be completely obvious what she was doing to him, since his towel had become more like a tent. "It's sort of a direct ratio thing," Hawk murmured in his own defense.

Her eyes lifted to his, wide and questioning.

"The longer you look at me like that, the more turned on I get."

"Oh." She grinned.

He tried to laugh, and found his mouth touching her temple.

She lifted her face and their noses bumped. "Oh," she said again, even more breathlessly, and then he was stroking away her hair, which was poking him in the eye.

She smiled a little, but her gaze was glued to his mouth, which was a mere fraction of an inch from hers, and then suddenly she'd closed the gap. When her tongue met his, he thought he'd died and gone to heaven. Oh, God, he didn't want her to ever stop.

Cupping the back of her head with his hand, he deepened the kiss, which tugged a surprised, throaty moan from her and sent a flood of desire raging through him, one that seriously threatened the placement of his towel. Abby was curvy and warm in his arms, her soft sighs of pleasure causing a rush of emotion that nearly swamped him.

She had one hand on his chest, palm open, as if she might have originally planned on holding him off but had lost her train of thought.

Or changed her mind.

He hoped for that second option. She was battling her demons, and Hawk could appreciate that because he had his own. All his life, his job had always taken priority, over family, over friends, over everything. While in Special Forces, he'd lost most of those close to him because it was hard to maintain relationships with what he did for a living.

He'd felt a little regret—but there'd always been that elusive future when he'd stop working, settle down and get serious about letting someone in his life. For now, he was still driven to ferret out bad guys. Hell, he didn't even *know* how to do anything else, be anyone else. Women as a whole didn't seem to like that, and as a result, they'd come and gone, mostly gone.

But when Abby looked at him, he didn't have to try to downplay his life, or hide how crazy his job was. She knew, because she lived it, too.

So freeing. Slipping his fingers into her hair, Hawk kissed her again, deeper now, trying to let her know it was okay to delve as long and hot and wet as she wanted. With a sexy-as-hell little murmur, she lifted one of her hands.

Oh, yeah, he thought. Touch me. *Do it.* Even the thought made him hard. Or harder, because he'd been hard, painfully so, since he'd pulled her onto the bed with him.

Her hand hovered in the air, then headed toward his shoulder, touched down, jerked back, then touched down again.

At the connection, he groaned and she jerked both hands off him and pulled her mouth free, lips wet, breathing ragged, body trembling. "I'm sorry," she gasped.

Sorry? Was she kidding? "No, I want you to—" Wanted so much he was afraid to even finish the thought. But she'd kissed him like he was better than air, like he was her lifeline, her only hope, like maybe that one kiss wasn't going to be enough, could never be enough.

Yeah, he could live off that fantasy alone. When he'd rolled around with her on that hard ground at the ranch, her body had moved against his, all curves and softness, and he'd sent up a desperate wish that someday they'd be rolling around and *not* fighting for their lives.

The need had surprised him then, but it didn't now. This thing between them had been building up for six months, six months during which he'd been frustrated and hot and bothered, and he hoped she'd been the same. Now there was nothing to hold them back.

Still staring at him with those wide eyes, Abby lifted her fingers to her mouth and slowly shook her head. "I'm sorry. I'm not ready—"

"Okay," he managed. He even smiled, though truthfully, he wanted to cry. "It's okay."

"It's just that you're so strong," she said very softly, staring at the width of his shoulders. His chest. The tattoo on his bicep. His belly…the tented towel. "Very strong."

That clearly was not a compliment. "Would it help to know that when you look at me, I feel like a two-pound weakling?"

She smiled, but shook her head. Hawk sighed. He *was* strong. Hell, he'd spent years toning and strengthening his body for his job, they both knew that. It'd been a matter of survival after all. "I'd never use my strength against you, Abby."

"Except, of course, if I was going to turn you in."

At the reminder of how he'd tumbled her around in the woods, he winced. "I tried really hard not to—"

"I know. And you weren't naked then, and I couldn't really see…but now…" She lifted a shoulder. "I guess I'm just wishing that you were very skinny, or maybe even fat. Yeah, fat would do."

He blinked. "You'd rather I was fat?"

"And weak. Instead of…" She eyeballed him again. "You know."

"Wow. Okay…"

"I'm sorry."

"No, wait. I can fix this." Grabbing the handcuffs on the nightstand, he snapped one on his wrist, the other to the headboard.

Abby stared at him in shock. "What are you doing?"

Arm stretched above his head now, he leaned back. "Just sitting here. Not fat, sorry, but weakened. One hand only, see?" Hawk wriggled his fingers. "You can take me one-handed, and we both know it. I'm at your mercy, Ab." He looked into her eyes. "You're in total control."

Something leaped into her gaze at that, gratitude, relief, and oh, baby, a whole bunch of heat that had his own blood boiling again. His fingers itched to move, to touch her, but he remained still as stone.

Well, except for the part of him that he couldn't make go still. Beneath the towel it gave a hopeful surge.

Her gaze dropped to it.

"Okay, well that part of me has a mind of its own. But the rest of me? Just sitting here. Restrained. So do as you will, Abby. Look, touch…" Taste. "Whatever you want, I'm yours."

Totally.

Completely.

Yours.

Obviously intrigued, she reached out to touch his chest, then pulled back. "But…?"

"But what? No buts."

"But what happens when we're back in the real world?"

"Now see, I sort of thought we *were* in the real world."

"You know what I mean," Abby protested. "The real world is different. We work together in the real world. We have to be professional."

"Hey, I'm the king of professional."

She laughed. *Laughed.* And it was the sweetest sound he'd ever heard. Then she leaned a hand on his chest, bracing her weight completely over him as she peered into his face. "You're going to stay just like this? Really?"

"Just like this."

If it killed him.

Which it might.

"It's not that I'm afraid of you…."

"I know."

"I'm just…"

"You need the control. It's okay, Ab. I get it." He

jangled the handcuff to remind her how much he got it. She hadn't been sexually abused, but being stripped, helpless, had left its mark. They'd destroyed her confidence. They'd hurt her.

Now the situation was reversed.

She had a chance to be the one clothed, the one with all the power, and he was going to sit there and let her do whatever she wanted. "You're in the driver's seat."

"What should I do?" she whispered.

"Whatever you want."

"To you?"

"To me."

She stared into his eyes, torn between wariness and excitement. Just seeing it had his body leaping.

Down boy. He offered her a smile. "Just be kind."

"I will," she said very seriously, as if taking care with him was of the utmost importance, and for some reason that reached out and grabbed him by the throat. In his life, he was the one who took care of others, making places safe, taking out the bad guys...

But few, if any, had ever taken care of him, or even wanted to.

There Abby sat, fully dressed, her lower lip between her teeth as she contemplated him, arm stretched above his head, handcuffed to the bed in just a towel. As he waited there, not moving, hell barely breathing, she didn't move either.

But she was thinking, thinking so loudly he could practically hear her mind racing. Her face was flushed, and he could see her nipples pressing against the material of her shirt, two tight, aching peaks just waiting their turn for attention, which he was dying to give.

"I'm not sure where to start," she admitted.

He could guide her, even rush her. Everything in those wide eyes, in the way she was breathing, told him he could.

But he'd promised her all the control, promised her that she could go at whatever pace she wanted. And if she wanted more, and Hawk hoped like hell she wanted more, she needed to make this first move. "Wherever you want."

"Okay." Finally she lifted a hand and glided it over his chest, her finger brushing one of his nipples.

His muscles leaped, and feeling it, she paused, then arched an eyebrow and did it again. "You like that."

He was already sweating. "Yes."

Chewing on her lower lip in great concentration, she ran her hands down his torso. More quivering on his part. "And that," she noted. "You like that, too."

"Let me save you some time here," he managed. "I'm going to like everything you do."

"Really?" Again her fingers moved, lower.

Over his ribs.

Then his trembling abs.

All while she watched his face with great interest.

Hawk had fantasized about this and far, far more. But in those X-rated dreams, he'd completely under-estimated the effect she would have on him. Hell, she didn't even have to be touching him to make him hard, just the sound of her voice could do it, and yet now she was pressed to his side, looking, touching…

Stay still, he reminded himself.

The hardest thing he'd ever done.

"Okay," she whispered, answering some un-spoken question in her own head. Then she dipped her head and nearly, but not quite, touched her lips to his.

And then stopped.

He didn't move either, just did his best to keep breathing so he wouldn't pass out and miss some-thing good.

And then, as if he'd somehow passed a final test he hadn't even seen coming, she licked her lips and kissed him.

Killed him.

Same thing.

15

Cheyenne Memorial Hospital

CALLEN SAT AT LOGAN'S SIDE. She'd been watching over the cocky ATF agent as she often watched over her patients, with one noticeable difference.

Her heart was in her throat.

Not a comfortable place for it to be, not for a person who was used to being in charge at all times. But all sense of control had deserted her. So had common sense. And for what? The one thing she'd always sworn she'd keep her head about.

A man.

His partner's call had shaken her to the core. Logan was in danger; it sounded crazy, but she'd believed him. So much so that she'd switched the charts, and now Logan was Stephen Caudill. At the next shift change, he'd be making yet another chart change.

To Annabelle Levin, a thirty-year-old woman, nine months pregnant, five centimeters dilated.

He'd be so thrilled.

God. She'd risked all tonight. For a man. Her sister would not be happy. Kate had raised Callen because their parents had been hardly more than kids themselves, and not the sharpest tools in the shed, either. And she had warned Callen—*when love hits, it's like a ton of bricks upside the head. Either wear a helmet or accept that at some point, you're going to get clobbered.*

Heeding those words, Callen had made her way through life without getting overly involved.

Until now. Now she'd been clobbered, and as tough as she was, as careful as she'd been, she'd had no warning.

Kate had been right. It made no sense, and Callen had no explanation for it, but Logan was The One.

She knew it.

And she'd been so careful with her heart, too, only giving it away when she was quite certain it was safe.

Ha! Now she'd handed it over to an ex–Special Forces ATF agent who was currently embroiled in a situation where some high-ranking official wanted him dead. Just about as unsafe as it got.

But, good God, the man had charisma in spades. All he had to do was look at her. Hell, even lying there prone and far too still, she felt the space around her heart constrict, making it almost painful to be near him.

How did that happen in a matter of hours?

And then there'd been his obvious connection to his partner, and the frank concern he'd felt over leaving him alone to face the mess they'd found themselves in. She'd always had a thing for a man with a hero complex, and this man was definitely hero complex worthy.

She watched his face for signs of pain, because that she could handle, there she knew what to do, but his eyes were closed, his drool-inducing body motionless.

He was out cold.

So why her heart pounded, she had no clue. She couldn't seem to find her cool reserve, the place in her head where she kept her fears and panic at bay. There she could treat and care for the sickest of people, and still remain a little bit distant, just enough that she didn't lose a piece of her heart to each and every person who came into her life.

Because a lot of needy people came into her life.

But with Logan she hadn't been able to retreat. It wasn't just his physical attributes. She was immune to good looks and easy charm; in her line of work, she'd seen both erased by pain and suffering, leaving only the soul beneath.

Maybe it was his wit, which in spite of the pain, he'd shown in spades. Or maybe it had been the way he'd looked at her, as if she was the only woman he'd ever really seen.

Yeah, Callen thought, letting out a shaky breath. That'd been it.

She sat, at his side, watching him sleep as if she could keep him alive by willing it. But his injuries weren't going to kill him, he was merely sleeping off the pain and the load of meds he'd been given. By daylight he'd open those melting eyes and be on his way to recovery.

And then she'd go.

Deep in his drug-induced dreamland, Logan let out a long sigh. He could be dreaming about anything, she knew, given the dangerous life he led. Shifting closer, she set her hand on his arm and stroked, hoping her touch was soothing. "Don't let the bad dreams get you."

"I'm not asleep."

She nearly jumped out of her skin.

Turning his arm, he snagged her fingers in his. "Sorry."

He had a cut on his thumb and his palm was rough, callused. Warm. Leaning over him, she looked into his eyes. "Why aren't you sleeping?"

"Fighting the drugs." His voice was low, raw. Rough. "Callen—"

"Right here."

"If the worst happens—"

"Hold it." Her stomach dropped. "The worst is not going to happen."

A ghost of a smile touched his lips. "If you really believed that, you wouldn't have changed my chart."

Damn.

"I just want you to know," he murmured. "I could have fallen for you. The can't-eat-can't-sleep-can't-do-any-fucking-thing kind of fall."

Well, if that didn't grab her by the throat. She swallowed. "That's the drugs talking."

"Hell if it is." He lifted his arm, revealing the fact that he'd pulled out his IV.

The man was fighting a massive concussion,

three fractured ribs and a wrecked leg, with no drugs. "Logan—"

"I want you to believe me. I could have fallen in love with you."

Her eyes filled. "Shut up and save it, because no one's dying."

He tried to smile but failed. "Shit."

"Damn it, let me redo the IV."

"No. I'm good. I'm still breathing, remember? Tell me again what Hawk said."

"You need to rest."

"I'll rest when I'm dead. Listen, I know he needs help—"

"You need help. And I'm here to give it."

"No. I'm not dragging you into this any more than I already have. I can handle this. You need…you need to go."

He said this with his eyes still closed, and he held onto her hand as if he didn't intend to ever let go. "Callen?"

She couldn't tear her gaze from his face. "Yes?"

He licked his dry lips. A decidedly un-nurse-like longing filled her. "You're still here."

"Yeah."

"Why?"

"Because I'm a nurse."

"That's not why."

She was glad he hadn't opened his eyes. "Maybe I don't want you to wake up alone. Why were you faking sleep?"

"Honestly?" He finally opened his eyes. "I was

waiting for you to leave so I could break out of this joint."

She stared at him. Laughed. "Come on."

He didn't smile.

"Logan. You're not going anywhere."

"Want to bet?"

Her smile faded. "You're not kidding."

"Hawk needs me, Callen."

"He's going to have to wait for you, then. And don't even think about shaking your head, it'll hurt like hell."

"Jesus," he gasped, and lay back. "Okay, you're right."

"There, now see? You just keep saying things like that, and we'll be good."

Logan laughed, low and a bit hoarse. "What the hell are we doing?"

"About your health? I don't know, but I'm prepared to sit on you if that's what it takes to keep you here."

Swiveling his head, he looked right into her eyes, his own suddenly heated in spite of all the pain he must be feeling. "Maybe I'll try to get up so you can do just that."

"Probably sleeping would be a better use of your time." Callen managed to sound normal in spite of the fact her entire body had reacted to his words. The man was a walking, talking sex toy. But she had a vibrator, thank you very much, and didn't require a man for such simple pleasures as sex.

Although it'd been awhile, maybe she wasn't remembering it clearly.

"I can't sleep," he said. "I can't do anything but think about what I should be doing."

Logan needed a distraction. So many inappropriate things came to mind she had to stand up and flick on the television.

"What's that?" he asked.

She glanced up at the screen. *"Friends."*

"I meant what are you doing?"

"Distracting you from trying to break out of this joint, when you're still so hurt you can't even take a deep breath."

Reaching out, he snagged her hand. "Looking at you is distraction enough. You're so pretty, Callen."

"Stop it." But his words did something they shouldn't have, they warmed her from the inside out. "You're just trying to charm me into complacency so you can get out of here."

That he didn't deny that sent a frisson of alarm up her spine. He was. He was still going to try to get out of here and head back into danger.

"How many patients like me have you had to babysit since you've been a nurse?"

"Like you?" She laughed. "Exactly none. You're fairly different." As in off-the-charts different.

"I don't want to watch TV," he whispered, and very, very carefully, he sat up.

"You're not leaving."

"Callen—"

"I'll stop you," she warned.

He eyed her. "How?"

Good question. She opened her big old purse that

held just about everything except a kitchen sink and sifted through for inspiration. She pulled out the book she'd planned on reading tonight if there'd been a break.

Logan took a look at the nearly naked earl on the cover, the one pulling off some maiden's dress, and laughed. "Okay, but could you skip to the good parts?"

Hmm, maybe not reading. Again, she searched the depth of the purse and came up with a pair of playing cards.

"I'm not a big card player."

She was running out of options. "Are you telling me you're not a gambling man?"

That caught his interest. "Poker? You'd take advantage of a man when he's down?"

If that's what it took. "What's the matter, you chicken?"

His eyes heated with the challenge. "Lock the door."

"What?" She laughed, though inside something leaped to attention. "Why?"

"Because if we're playing poker, we're going to do it right. Lock the door, Callen."

As if she was having an out-of-body experience, she got up and locked the door. "This is crazy."

"Now who's chicken?"

"You're suggesting we play strip poker?"

His eyes flashed. "I hadn't suggested anything. But since you've brought it up, sounds great. I'm in."

She opened her mouth, then closed it again, not

wanting to analyze the way her bones felt sort of loose, and her skin too tight. At least he was no longer thinking about breaking out of this joint….

Oh, God. She was actually going to do this. Good thing she had a great poker face and was incredibly lucky. Not to mention fully dressed, while he had on a hospital gown and nothing else. It was a win-win situation for her. "Five card stud," she said, shuffling. "Deuces wild."

"I'm beginning to think that's not all that's wild."

Her gaze met his. "If in the end—"

"You mean when you're naked."

"Actually, I meant when *you're* naked." Just the words brought an illogical thrill, since she'd already seen everything there was to see when they'd cut off his clothes. Except that hadn't counted because at the time she'd actually been working on him, and truly had been focused on that. She wanted another peek, and the time to enjoy it. "If I win," she went on, "you stay here."

"And if *I* win…"

He paused and Callen felt like she was on the edge of a cliff, with her toes hanging off, a wind blowing at her back, and the earth rocking and rolling beneath her. "If you win, what?"

He full out grinned. "Winner's choice."

"You're not going to name it?"

"I'm going to keep it a surprise."

Oh, God. Okay. No problem. She pretended like that hadn't gone straight to all her good spots, and dealt the cards. A pair of tens. Not great, but not bad. She looked at him. He had no expression on his face whatsoever, and asked for two more cards. She took three.

And got a deuce. Oh, yeah. She kept her grin to herself and let him call her. "Three of a kind," she said, and fanned out the cards to show him.

He nodded, and with absolutely no expression on his face, revealed his hand—a full house.

Callen stared down at the cards in silence. Oh, boy. "Well," she finally said, and stood. "That was fun, but maybe this episode of *Friends* is a good one—"

"You have to lose an item of clothing."

Right. No problem. She pulled off her scrub top. Beneath she wore a pink bra. More coverage than her bikini, really, but here in this hospital room, with the light on dim, she felt extremely…naked.

He let his gaze dip from hers and slowly took her in, from the scar on her shoulder—result of rotator cuff surgery several years back—to her belly ring, to her hard nipples.

And it wasn't cold in the room. Quite the opposite, actually.

After a long, charged moment, he let out a long breath. "Consider me distracted."

Yeah, her, too. She reached for the cards and shuffled. Dealt. Stared at her hand without seeing a thing, because he hadn't taken his eyes off her, and it was all she could do to breathe.

Nothing could happen. He was too injured, and they were in a hospital room for God's sake…and yet she'd never felt so aroused in her entire life.

He took two cards, and so did she, both of them inhaling just a little too heavily, the silence so charged she could almost see the current sparking between them.

The only item of clothing he had to lose was his gown. She still had her scrub bottoms and bra and panties to strip, and suddenly the idea of doing that held far more appeal than winning.

Logan was looking into her eyes, not at his cards, waiting for her move.

"Call," she whispered, her voice tight.

Without breaking eye contact, he revealed…a pair of fives.

She set the cards face down and stood.

"What did you have?" he asked.

A pair of jacks. Which beat him, but she wasn't going to mention that.

"Callen?"

"You win." Gaze locked on his, she pulled on the tie of her scrub bottoms and let them fall.

He stared at her panties with the U.S. flag on the little triangle of material and let out a breath. "God bless America."

A shaky laugh escaped her.

"You take my breath, Callen."

"That's your injuries."

"No, it's you. Come here."

"Our game isn't over. I'm trying to make sure you're good and distracted."

"Oh, I'm good and distracted, all right. All the blood has drained south for the winter. Please come here."

Her feet took her forward until her thighs bumped Logan's bed.

He tossed back his covers, revealing his wrapped leg, the hospital gown, and pressing against it...

A most impressive erection. "Oh, my," she whispered.

"Yeah, unfortunately I can't move, so there's not much I can do with it."

She wanted to tell him he didn't have to move, that she'd do all the work.

Oblivious to where her thoughts had gone, he patted the spot next to him. And then she did as she'd never imagined she'd actually do. She climbed into bed with him and slid into his arms as if she'd been made for them.

Putting her face into his throat, she wrapped her arms carefully around his neck and just breathed him in. "This is new," she admitted.

"Cuddling in a hospital bed?"

"Cuddling. Period."

"I knew it. You're a serial heartbreaker, aren't you? A love 'em and leave 'em kind of woman. Damn." Logan sighed with mock hurt. "Be kind to me, will you?"

Her heart absolutely melted, and she knew she planned on being anything he wanted.... Lifting her head, Callen held his gaze while she reached behind her for her purse.

"What are you doing?"

She unzipped an inside pocket and pulled out a—

"Condom." He stared at it, then her. "Callen. Are you sure—"

"Very."

He took it from her, then let out a frustrated breath. "I'm going to hate myself for saying this, but I don't think I can—"

"No, but I can."

Logan stared into her eyes as she pulled the sheet, and then his hospital gown, from his body. He let her see every reaction as it hit him—arousal, hunger, desire, all for her…. And when she was finished, they were both sweating a little, both laughing a little, even before she carefully straddled him, slipping her panties to one side so she could slide down over him without hurting his leg.

"Ah, God, Callen…" he said roughly. She hugged his hips with her inner thighs and lifted up, until he was nearly out of her, before sinking back onto him.

Heaven. On. Earth. Her eyes drifted shut as she rocked on him, moving her own hands down her body.

"No," he whispered, voice hoarse. "Stay with me."

Startled, she opened her eyes. Arching backward, she fisted her hands in the bedsheets to avoid accidentally touching his chest and jarring his ribs. "Yeah," he murmured. "Like that." As she continued to move on him so that he slid in and out of her in a dizzying rhythm, Logan danced his good hand up her damp body, cupping a breast, rasping his thumb over her nipple, then gliding over her ribs, her belly, and lower, where they were connected, gently stroking, stroking…until she was coming completely undone for him.

Completely.

Undone.

She only vaguely heard his broken groan as he followed her over.

Wow. Just…wow…

"Callen," he whispered a long moment later as they both slowly came back to themselves.

She separated their bodies, realizing that he probably needed to breathe, and went to dismount from the bed, but he tightened his hand on her arm and drew her down beside him.

"Don't." He nuzzled at her neck, sounding sleepy, and so sexy she wanted another go at him. "Don't leave."

No. No, given the danger he was in, she wouldn't. And a small part of her was grateful for the excuse to stay. She curled up as he drifted off, feeling the last of the tension drain out of her limbs.

It'd been an incredible day: nerve-wracking, terrifying and exhilarating all at once, and she sighed, exhaustion creeping up on her as well. She'd let her defenses down with this one, and no doubt she was heading toward Hurt City, but right now in his arms, sated, content, she didn't care.

16

THE HOTEL ROOM WAS WARM, COZY and shockingly intimate, but that wasn't what caught Abby's breath. No, that came from the sight of Hawk, naked except the towel, stretched out for her perusal.

Or for whatever she chose.

Handcuffed to the headboard, eyes dark and full and steady on hers, he made quite the sight. If she thought too much about what she'd like to do to him, she'd probably die of embarrassment.

So she didn't think.

She just did. "I saw you," she whispered. "That first day on the job, without a shirt. I wanted to touch."

"That would have worked for me."

"But I didn't know you then."

His eyes met hers. "And you think you know me now?"

"Yes."

"I'm not talking about the ATF part, Abby."

"Me either."

"Most people don't see past that, you know."

Something in his careful tone caught her. Softened her. "Yes," she whispered. "I can see why. As an ATF agent, you're pretty impressive. But that's not what draws me to you."

Again, his gaze met hers, and for the first time ever, she saw a hint of vulnerability. She thought maybe that was the most arousing thing about him, even though he was built like a pagan statue, all golden skin stretched taut over defined muscle.

Like her, he wasn't good at showing people what was beneath the exterior. Probably that drew her more than anything.

He had scars, lots of them, some old and some very new. A dark bruise bloomed over his ribs. Several inches below that, he had another on his hipbone, partially hidden by the towel.

She found herself wanting to touch each and every single one. So she reached out and lightly put the pad of her finger to one of his pecs. He made a low sound and went very still, so very carefully still she knew he was exercising every bit of control he had. She was running the show, and he wanted her to know it.

A rush of gratitude and warmth flooded her at that. He understood.

People had tried to understand in the past year. Friends. Family.

Men.

Gaines had tried to understand, had claimed to get it, and yet there'd remained something far too aggressive about him, and she hadn't been able to get past that.

Hawk, too, was a big, bad, aggressive alpha guy, through and through. In work, in play, even in rest, everything about him suggested that he could be ready for anything in a blink of an eye.

And yet he hadn't aimed that aggression at her. Hell, he hadn't even done so when she'd been wrestling him down to the ground in the midst of explosions and fire. He'd rolled her beneath him, yes. He'd held her down, yes. But never to simply exert his superior strength over her.

Now he'd given her free rein to do as she would to him. And, God, the things she wanted to do… She'd started out at his side, but somehow after she'd kissed him, she'd ended up sprawled out, half on top of him. Abby could feel the power of him beneath her, latent, edgy power, all contained and controlled. It was intoxicating. It made her tingly and uncomfortably hot.

He made her feel…sensual. Yeah, that was it. He made her feel sexy in a way she hadn't expected to feel again, at least not now, not with him.

So she kissed him again. He was aroused, she could feel that, too, nudging at her hip, and instead of worrying her, she felt a rush of excitement. Real, true lust. She was damp with it, even. Their mouths were touching, they were breathing each other's air, but it wasn't enough.

She opened her eyes and found his open as well, filled with heat, patience and amusement.

"What's so funny?" she asked.

He gave a shake of his head. "I thought I was dead tonight. Several times. But that was nothing to this."

"What do you mean?"

"You're killing me, Abby. Killing me with your sweetness, your heat—no, don't stop."

She'd begun to pull away, but saw that he wasn't making fun of her.

He wanted her to keep going.

And shockingly, she wanted to do just that. Cupping his face, she slid her finger along his rough jaw, tilting it a little before kissing him again.

"Deeper," he urged so very softly she might have imagined it. She opened her mouth, then ran her tongue along his lower lip, an action that wrenched a guttural groan from him. His free hand came up, gripping the headboard next to his bound one, as if he didn't trust himself not to touch her. But she trusted him, so she did as he'd asked and deepened the kiss, getting a little lost in the heat of him, in the taste, in the way they were moving.

And then she found she yearned for his hands on her. "Hawk, touch me."

"Abby—"

"Please? Touch me."

He let go of the headboard to stroke his hand down her back in a languid, sensual motion that had her stretching and nearly purring like a cat. She'd missed this. Being touched. Although she couldn't ever remember a man's touch making her want to melt into a puddle at his feet. Needing more, she kissed him again and his fingers tightened on her shirt, fisted in the material at the small of her back, urging her a little closer.

When she ran her tongue along his, he made a low sound and slid his hand beneath her shirt. His fingers were callused, and his touch curled her toes as they stroked up and down, catching on her bra strap. And then somehow she was fully on top of him, kissing him wildly, spiraling out of control.

With another of those low sexy noises deep in his throat, he rocked his hips to hers, nestling his erection against her core. Surprised, she jerked.

"Sorry," he gasped, and pulled back, removing his hand from beneath her shirt, slapping it back on the headboard next to his bound one, face tight, body tighter. *"Sorry."*

"No—"

"I'm going to close my eyes," he said in a hoarse voice, doing just that. "It might help if I can't see how you look sitting there touching me, the feel of you on my skin, the look on your face as it hits you what that touch is doing to me—" He winced. "Christ. Even my own words are turning me on."

"Hawk, I'm not that fragile."

"I know."

"I just didn't know if I was ready for this—"

"I know that, too. It's okay, I have a grip now." A white-knuckled one. "Let's try again."

Abby wanted to. More than anything. Because something had occurred to her. She felt no sense of panic, no claustrophobia at all as she let her fingers fall from his jaw, over his throat, down his chest, damp now, and rising and falling more quickly than when he'd run through the woods. She skimmed his abs, those amazing, sexy abs, which she wanted to trace with her tongue, then touched the edge of the towel where it was tucked into itself. It loosened.

Gaped away from those abs.

And her mouth watered. "Hawk, can I—"

"Anything," he said hoarsely, his eyes closed, his Adam's apple bouncing as he swallowed hard. "Any-god-damn-thing you want."

Biting her lower lip, she scooted back on his thighs so that she could bend down and press her mouth to his chest.

Feminine power surged through her, and she opened her mouth and licked him. He let out another rough sound but didn't move. She watched as his nipples puckered.

Hers did the same.

And then, almost without her brain's approval, her fingers tugged on his towel. It slipped free, and then *whoops*, look at that, spread wide, falling away from him.

"Oh," she breathed. He was bigger than she'd imagined. Just looking at him made her thighs tingle, and between them, much more than tingle. The sensation felt so wondrous, she went very quiet to savor every single second. Then she wrapped her hand around him.

A strangled sound tumbled from his lips, but he held still.

Warm metal. That's what he felt like. "You're big all over," she noted a bit shakily.

A harsh laugh escaped him. "Normally, I'd take that as a compliment, but—christ, Abby!"

She'd bent over and kissed him, on the very tip. "Do we have a condom?" she asked, then nibbled him again.

Another wordless sound rumbled from his chest, and his body arched up from the mattress, seeking her lips. "Bathroom," he gasped. "Basket on the counter."

She rushed into the bathroom, staring for one beat at the rosy, sensual woman in the mirror, then raced back to Hawk, galvanized by the golden, sinewy body stretched before her, flexed and taut with need. "Hawk."

"I know." He gulped in air and quivered. "I swear I'm trying to just sit here—"

"I need the key." Abby climbed back onto the bed. "I need you to touch me with both hands."

His head whipped up, his eyes connecting with hers. "Are you sure—"

"Yes."

Nearly before she'd gotten the word out, he'd grabbed the key on the nightstand and freed himself, his hands immediately going to her hips, pulling her over him. Feeling him beneath her brought a rush of heat and more excitement, and, helplessly, she rocked her hips, frustrated by her clothes.

"How do you want me to touch you?" His hands danced up her ribs, his fingers not quite touching her breasts, though they ached for him to. "Here?" His thumbs scraped lightly over her belly.

Now *her* head fell back, and with her hips in

motion, slowly rocking, oscillating, she was nothing but a bundle of raw nerve endings, racing toward the finish line.

"Abby?"

"Everywhere."

His fingers reached for the buttons on her shirt, and for a moment, she froze, because, oh, yeah, this was where she'd have to get naked…

In the warm circle of light from the lamp, his gaze met hers. "Just me, remember?"

"I know." She did, she really did, but she'd liked this a lot better when she wasn't thinking about losing her clothes.

So gently it nearly brought tears to her eyes, Hawk cupped her face. "We can stop here, Ab. I'll probably cry but we can stop."

She smiled, as he'd meant her to.

"Yeah," he whispered. "Love that look on you. Trust me Abby…."

Oh, God, she really wanted to, but she wasn't ready to bare herself, and she couldn't force that. Twisting, she wrestled with a shoe, finally kicking it and one leg of her pants off before straddling him again.

"Wait. Abby, wait—" His hands on her waist tightened as he looked down her legs, opened over his thighs, at what she'd exposed. "Oh, God, look at you—"

"I need you inside me, Hawk."

"God, you're beautiful. So wet." Lightly, oh so devastatingly lightly, he stroked a thumb over her, right where she wanted him to sink into her body.

"Now," she nearly sobbed. "Please now."

"Yes, all of it, but first—" He stroked her, right at the center of her world, making her tremble, making her pant for air while with his other hand, he began to skim up her top, leaning in as if he planned on putting his mouth on the places he exposed.

Only she didn't want to be exposed, didn't want to tremble. She didn't want his tender gentleness now, she wanted him inside her, pounding until she exploded, until this desperate, almost unbearable tension left her. So she rose up on her knees and sank down over him—

"Abby, Jesus. Wait—"

Not stopping until he was fully seated within her.

17

BURIED DEEP INSIDE ABBY, the woman of his dreams, Hawk gripped her hips and tried to keep a grip on himself as well.

She hadn't removed any of her clothing except the absolute essentials to get him inside her. She'd barely let him touch her, and certainly hadn't let him put his mouth on her, which he was absolutely dying to do.

Nope, she just wanted to get to the big bang, and you know what? He was going to let her. He was going to let her do whatever she damn well wanted to do to get off, and then, when she was soft and sated and damp and dewy, he had plans, big ones. He'd lay her back, strip her out of those clothes she was using as armor, tasting every inch he exposed, making her forget every nightmare she'd had over the past year, everything but this.

Him.

Even his thoughts were making him hot, and he pushed up deep inside her, and, oh, God, yeah, his groan co-mingled with hers, a sound that was music to his ears. She was right there with him. Not lost in unhappy memories, but here, with him. To keep her so, he slid his hands forward on her thighs, urging her up again, guiding her nearly off him before letting go so that she sank back down, panting in a matching rhythm that shot right through him.

Again she did it, while rocking those hips, setting him on fire. Staying still was all but impossible now, and he pushed up inside her, deep as he could get, and nearly lost it right then and there.

Leaning over him, she fisted her hands on his chest, getting a few chest hairs in the mix, but, hey, she could rip them all out one by one for all he cared. He wanted to watch her come undone for him, listen to her cry out his name, feel her spasm around him and know he'd brought her there. Sliding a hand through her hair, he tilted her head back, exposing her sweet neck, which he kissed, making his way down to her collar. Nudging it aside as far as he could, he licked her skin, then dipped his head and kissed her breast through the material of her shirt and bra.

"No," she gasped. "No, I just want to—" She broke off with a frustrated sob, her hips rocking, arching, her hair in her face, her skin damp and over-heated. "Please, I just need to—"

Come. She was so desperate to get there that she was blocking herself. "Abby." He slid his hands to her hips and slowed her down, meeting her thrust for thrust, but going deeper now, harder, more controlled.

"I can't—"

"I'm hard as a rock," he murmured, kissing her jaw, her throat. "You do that to me. Can you feel me?"

Panting, she nodded.

Dipping his head, he rubbed his jaw over her breast, teasing the nipple through her shirt. "You do it for me, Abby. Completely. Let me do it for you."

"I can't—"

Pushing up her shirt, he rasped his tongue over her nipple.

She let out a sweet, shuddering sigh, and tried to move her hips faster again but he was holding them now, coaxing her to a slower rhythm, where she'd feel. Every. Single. Thing.

"Hawk," she whispered, clinging to him as if making sure he wouldn't let go.

He wouldn't. Ever. "Right here…"

She was panting again, warm and sweet and soft, murmuring his name over and over in his ear. The sound was the most erotic, most sensual, most heart-felt thing he'd ever heard, and just a little terrifying.

She felt it, too.

"Hawk?"

"Right here with you," he promised, breathing with her as he thrust up deep inside her, loving the feel of her breasts pressed to his chest, her thighs hugging his. His hands slipped down, cupping her ass, pulling her in, absorbing her soft gasp with his mouth.

She was going to come for him now, he could feel it in the desperate clutch of her hands, could see it in the way her eyes turned glossy and opaque. And then, with his name on her lips, she shattered, her body shuddering in his arms with so much sweet bliss it triggered his own release, dragging him under the wave of searing pleasure with her. He plunged into her one last time, trembling as he came from the tips of his toes, from every cell in his body, from the depths of his heart.

And as he went over, he had one thought—God, don't let me fall in love.

Yet as his vision faded, as an almost painful heat poured through him endlessly, he knew that whatever it was, it was much, much more than simple lust.

ABBY CAME BACK TO HERSELF in slow degrees, lethargic, replete, and more sated than she had any right to be, given their situation.

She was sprawled over Hawk's lap, her pants hooked on one ankle, her shirt half-opened and one breast revealed, the tip of which he was absently rasping with one callused thumb.

She had her face plastered to his throat, and as she took stock, she was very glad he couldn't see her face. Her legs were spread wide over his, her hands clutching him as if she never intended to let him go free.

As for his hands, well, he'd gotten quite comfortable with her body, hadn't he. His other one was intimately gripping her bottom, lightly gliding over her skin, making her want to, even now, stretch like a damn kitten and expose her belly for more.

Good God.

His face was buried in her hair, and with a long, pleasure-filled sigh, he lifted his head. His eyes were heavy with sleep, and extremely sexy as he smiled at her, looking quite pleased with himself. "Hey."

"Hey." She had no idea what to do or say, a definite first.

"You okay?"

"I think you know damn well that I surpassed okay."

He grinned.

Oh, yes, very pleased with himself, wasn't he.

Tucking a strand of hair behind her ear, he let that finger do the talking, stroking it down her throat and over her bared shoulder, where it caught on her shirt.

"Maybe next time, we could lose a few clothes," he murmured.

"You're not wearing any."

"I meant you."

She looked down at her bedraggled self and sighed. "Yeah. I guess I stupidly thought that leaving them on would be like wearing armor."

His smile faded. "No stupid. You had quite a bit to overcome."

And speaking of that…she had come. Probably if he so much as touched her again, she could do it again in a blink. "I didn't expect it to be so…" She searched for a word, and failed to find one that suitably did the job. "Wow."

"Me either."

Okay, so she wasn't alone in that. That was good. It might have been a little more embarrassing if she had been.

"Abby?"

She worked on meeting his gaze.

"You don't need armor with me."

No. No, she hadn't. And if that wasn't completely unnerving, Abby had no idea what was. She held his sincere gaze and sighed again. "I know. But I also know we don't have time for this."

He looked as if he might argue, then nodded instead. "Sleep?"

"Shower first." And using that as a reason to escape, she got up, somehow managed to ignore the urge to cover her good parts, and headed to the bathroom mirror.

Oh, boy.

Her cheeks were rosy, her eyes glowing. And so was her body.

Who'd have thought that damn fine sex would be part of the cure?

Not just sex, she told herself as she got into the shower. She'd had a healthy sex life before the raid, and what she'd just done with Hawk, while very hot and very unexpected, wasn't it.

It was something much, much more.

Which made this the scariest part of the entire past twelve hours.

_18_

AFTER HER SHOWER, ABBY looked at her filthy clothes and sighed, then held up what Serena had brought her. A black and sparkly sweater, low cut. Jeans, which had been made to fit like a glove.

She turned back to her clothes, but yep, they were still disgusting. Worse, her panties had somehow ripped and were useless. With another sigh, she pulled on Serena's clothes, knowing she'd never fill them out the way their hostess did. But her goal here was survival, not winning a beauty contest.

Abby opened the bathroom door, and found herself hesitating. She was embarrassed at how she'd let go with Hawk, and wasn't sure she could handle looking at him.

He'd left a light on for her, and that alone was enough to warm her from the inside out. She opened her mouth to thank him, but closed it again.

Oh. My. Goodness.

There he was, right where she'd left him, sprawled face down on the bed.

Completely in the buff.

Eyes closed, back rising and falling with his deep breathing, he was out cold.

He hadn't even pulled the covers over him, not that she minded the chance to stand there and look her fill without him being aware of it. Good God, but the man had it going on. Legs that went on forever, long, sleek, smooth back, broad shoulders, rippled arms that knew exactly how to hold onto a woman….

And then there were the good parts. She let her eyes linger in all the NC-17 spots until he suddenly rolled to his back, one arm flung up and over his eyes. She spent another moment taking in the new and even better view.

"Are you going to get over here?" he murmured in a sleep-roughened voice. "Or just stare at me all night?"

Crap. "I, um…"

Eyes still closed, he patted the mattress at his side.

Her feet made the decision for her, carrying her across the room until the mattress bumped her thighs. Without looking, he unerringly flung out his hand and caught hers, pulling her down to his side. "Just an hour," he said, and tugged her into his arms, apparently unconcerned by the fact that once again he was naked and she fully dressed.

Well, it hadn't bothered him earlier, she told herself, and let herself relax into him. And not just relax, but press her face into his throat. She might have also inhaled deeply, and then snuggled even closer.

In response, he sighed with pleasure and ran his hands up and down her back in the most soothing gesture she'd ever experienced. So why her body tingled, suddenly hopeful that it was going to get another man-made orgasm, she had no idea.

"Still fully clothed," he murmured, and she could hear the smile in his voice.

Along with exhaustion. "Sleep," she ordered.

"I know…I am…" He snuggled in. "Abby?"

"Yeah?"

"Maybe next time, you could be naked, too…."

Yeah, she had to admit, lying skin to skin with him would be pretty damn amazing. "Maybe…"

He let out a shuddering sigh.

"Maybe even…" She was crazy. "Now…"

Another sigh, but no words.

Lifting her head, she stared down into his face.

He'd fallen back asleep.

The irony did not escape her. She was finally ready to shed the last of her armor, and what happened? The guy she was ready to share it with was dead to the world.

HAWK AND ABBY MADE IT INTO Cheyenne two hours and twelve minutes later. Hawk had allowed himself to pass out for an hour and a half before he'd gotten them back on the road.

Now they were in Serena's borrowed SUV, only a few miles from Abby's condo, and he still hadn't figured out a safe place to leave her while he retrieved her laptop. She'd adamantly refused to stay at the B&B. "Do you have family in the area?"

She turned and leveled him with those baby blues.

She wore Serena's clothes, and having discovered her ripped panties in the trash, he knew she was currently commando, a situation that was wreaking havoc with his thought process.

"Don't even think about ditching me."

"Maybe I was just asking." He did his best to put on his Sunday church face. The one that said he was an American hero, a man who'd never lie.

"My parents sold their house a few years back and retired to Florida," she said. "My sister moved there, too, with her kids."

"Sounds cozy."

"And too far for you to take me to."

He sighed, and dropped the innocent expression. "I just want you safe."

"If you're going to my condo, then so am I."

"If anyone's watching—"

"Then we move to Plan B."

This time the sound of the "we" didn't thrill Hawk. He couldn't stand the thought of how he'd dragged her into this entire disastrous mess.

She'd called Tibbs, briefly, letting him know she was alive and would be calling back with concrete evidence that would point to someone other than Hawk.

Where to take her?

"Stop trying to think of a place to dump me," she told him.

"Abby—"

"Look, don't make me use those handcuffs again."

He slanted her a look. "I might like that. Later."

She shook her head. "Men."

"Yeah. We're something."

"Something all right. What about *your* family?"

He glanced at her. "You going to ditch me now?"

A ghost of a smile crossed her mouth. "Maybe I'm just curious."

"My parents are gone."

"So you don't have family to be close with either."

"I have Logan." His heart squeezed just a little at the thought of what Logan was going through right about now. He'd called when they first hit the road, and Callen had promised she had him good and protected. Until he could get there, which would be right after he got the laptop, it would have to be good enough.

"Turn left here," Abby told him.

Her neighborhood was very suburban. Clean, cozy, sort of white picket fence meets the upscale set, complete with tennis court, pool, rec center... He wondered if she fit in here, and what she did on her time off. Did she wear a little white skirt and play tennis? Or slip into a bathing suit and swim laps?

"Up until last year, I never took any personal time for myself," she said as if she'd read his mind. "I was all work, work, work."

"And now?"

"Things have changed. I live my life. When I was on leave, I took tennis lessons. I could kick your ass all over that tennis court."

"Now that I'd like to see."

"Any time."

Her smug smile was the sexiest thing he'd ever seen. "I'm going to ask you to prove that one," he said.

"You play?"

"Well, it's been a while. In high school—"

She laughed. "I could take you."

"What do you wear when you play tennis?"

"What does that have to do with it?"

"Well, if it's a little tiny skirt, then I might have some trouble concentrating. I'll need a handicap."

She blinked, then smiled and shook her head, as if baffled.

"What?"

"You have this way of making me feel more like a woman in my grubbiest moments than I've ever felt in my entire life."

"Yeah, well, you have a way about you, too, Ab." Reaching for her hand, Hawk brought it up to his mouth. "Last night, I thought my life was over. Several times. You came through for me. I didn't realize it would be more than that, or that I'd get so much more than I bargained for. But I have."

"I'm more than you bargained for?"

"Hell, yeah. Aren't I for you? Isn't this?"

She stared at him, then let out a low laugh. "Wasn't even in the ballpark," she admitted. "But I can still take you on the court."

He laughed, suddenly feeling lighter than he could have imagined, given all they had in front of them. "You're on. You're so on."

If they lived.

"Take another left," she said. "Don't go to the gate."

They passed the front entrance, going around the

block. "Back way in." Abby pointed. "They're doing construction here, adding another park. The fence is down. If we walk in from there, there'll be no record of us entering."

Hawk liked how she thought. He liked how she did just about everything, including the way she stared at him, as if maybe he was worth a second, even a third look.

And he especially liked how she clutched him when he was buried so deep inside her he didn't know where he ended and she began.

Yeah, he liked *that* a lot.

"Park here," she said, jerking his thoughts out of bed, pointing to a handful of trucks. Construction trucks, by the looks of them, toolboxes and equipment in the back of each. "We'll fit right in."

"How about just me fitting in?"

"You want me to wait here?"

"Yes."

"No."

"Well, glad that's settled." They got out, and just as she'd said, no one stopped them. They walked over the downed fence, through the tall grass and trees that were being turned into a greenbelt area behind the condos, and right past the pool and tennis courts, directly into the courtyard along the back of the condo units.

"You shouldn't stay here during construction," he said. "It's not safe."

"A fact for which we're grateful, remember?"

No one paid them any attention as they walked the

length of the courtyard. Abby gestured to the second to last unit. "Home sweet home."

He stopped her at her back slider door and took her key. "Let me go in alone."

"For what, you to do the caveman thing and check the house?"

"Damn it. We're not going to fight about this, are we?"

She sighed. "We left the rifle in the car."

"Yes." He slid his hand up to her ponytail, lightly tugging her head back so he could cover her mouth with his for a short but effectively hot kiss.

"What was that for?" she asked, just a little breathless.

"You tend to stop arguing with me when I kiss you."

"It's because you're destroying my brain cells."

He ran his thumb over her lower lip.

She looked at the condo. "Hawk—"

"Look, what if I promise to argue with you later, your choice, will that work?"

Abby sighed again. "My laptop is on the little table by my bed, upstairs."

He let out a breath. "I'll be right back."

"Okay. And Hawk?"

He turned back. Her eyes met his, those full, irresistible orbs, and in them he saw something that made him swallow hard. Oh, God. *Don't say it,* he thought. Don't bring in the L-word, because I'm not going there. So far he'd managed to keep his heart intact.

But this time, with her, he wasn't sure he could keep it that way.

She smiled, and that organ he'd been protecting rolled over and exposed its belly. *Huh.* Maybe… maybe it wouldn't be such a bad thing to have someone love him, truly love him, the way few had ever done. Because looking into this woman's eyes, he could see a future, could almost admit he was ready for it. "Yeah?"

She patted his arm. "Watch the second step. It creaks."

GAINES THREW HIS CELL PHONE across his office, and all three men standing in the doorway ducked.

It hit his crystal clock and shattered. "I've got three loose ends," he said calmly, and looked down at his computer screen, from which all of Tibbs's communications transcripts blinked back at him.

Tapping into Tibbs's computer had been nothing short of genius, if he said so himself, as it allowed him to keep track of all the players and the events. *Win.* "We need to take care of them, or I'll take care of you."

"Sir, yes, sir. But Logan wasn't supposed to get transferred to the hospital," Benny said in their defense. Benny had worked beneath Watkins.

Had.

Watkins had become dispensable the moment he'd balked at taking care of Abby. He'd had no problem betraying Hawk, but when it came to a pretty woman, he hadn't had what it took.

Gaines, however, did.

"Logan should never have been transferred," Benny said again. "But Watkins—"

"*Is* dead." Gaines looked at each of them. "As you will be if you don't fix this." He turned back to the computer screen. Abby had called for her voice mail, from somewhere near the city limits. Somehow he just knew Hawk was with her. The knowledge that they'd taken seven hours to get into Cheyenne instead of the usual four told him that they'd stopped.

Probably slept.

Together?

No. No, deep down she had a thing for him, he was certain of it. He'd cultivated the hero worship in her, had carefully honed it. No, his Abby hadn't slept with Hawk. She was too cautious—as he knew all too well. How many months had he put into trying to get into her pants? He'd wined and dined the hell out of her, managing only a whole lot of restless nights.

Until the raid. Of course he'd been behind it. Mostly because she'd come damn close to exposing him, more by accident than design, but still. She was a smart cookie, and with a little more time she'd have figured it out.

He'd had to throw her off, at any cost. So he'd finagled a way to scare her and indebt her to him at the same time. Ingenious, if he said so himself. And yet he'd played the goddamn hero for her and she'd *still* not given it up for him.

Had she given it up for Hawk?

If so, it was only one more damn good reason to kill the son of a bitch. And then, unfortunately, her as well. It was going to disappoint him as much as it hurt her, but some things just had to be done….

Abby's condo complex

ABBY STOOD ON HER BACK PATIO, hidden behind a tall potted ficus, staring at the glass slider, but unable to see more than her own reflection.

The ficus needed watering.

Story of her life. Oh, she'd been a big talker back there in the SUV, telling Hawk that she was living her life.

Liar.

She was still hiding. Still keeping herself closed off to feelings. But she hadn't kept herself closed off to him, had she? Nope, she'd let him inside both her body and her heart. Come on in, steal the china. Sighing, she pressed her forehead to the potted tree and closed her eyes. What was she doing? Did she have any idea at all…?

No. No, she did not.

Lifting her head, she eyed the glass door again. Hawk had been gone just long enough to get up the stairs. Hawk, who'd put her life ahead of his.

Several times last night alone.

Last night…God, last night. It'd been the wildest night of her entire life. A shuddering sigh went through her. There'd been a moment, several of them, when she'd wanted to stay in his arms forever, as implausible as that wish had seemed.

Implausible and very, very unlikely.

It had just been one night. She was positive there'd been no more to it than fear and adrenaline and need, creating a desire she hadn't been able to ignore. Very soon now things would go back to the way they'd been.

And yet, some things would most certainly change. Her, for one. She'd forever be different for the experience, for discovering that she was every bit as strong as she'd hoped, that she could absolutely be a woman in every sense of the word. That maybe, just maybe, she could even learn to trust her heart again.

Had he entered her bedroom yet?

Had she made her bed?

Why was she standing out here wondering? Clearly, there was no trouble, she'd have heard something by now. Abby let herself inside. In the past, where she'd slept at night had never really been a home. She'd never had the time, nor the inclination to make one. But when she'd come here, she'd tried hard to create a haven, using warm colors, soft, cushy furniture and landscape photos of her favorite places on the walls.

She headed for the stairs, and in the doorway of her bedroom came face to face with the man who could both stop and kickstart her heart.

"Hey," Hawk said. "I heard you coming. I thought we decided you'd wait outside."

"No, you decided."

"Abby."

"Hawk." She repeated his tone, which made him laugh a little and reach for her.

She stepped right into his arms, and felt… amazing. Like she wasn't just standing in her home, she'd come home. Tilting her head back, she looked into his eyes, thinking she'd never had a man here, in this bedroom.

She'd never even given it a thought.

And yet this man, this quick-witted, smart, funny, sexy man, looked utterly and completely at home in her space.

It was a good fit.

"What?" he asked softly. "What is it?"

So damn much… "Later," she said.

Nodding slowly, he dipped his head and kissed her. Just a short, sweet kiss but their lips clung, and then opened, and then tongues got involved, and then…and then they were both panting and sort of arching into each other.

"The laptop," he murmured, his breath ragged, his hands beneath her shirt. "We're here for the laptop."

Right. With a steadying breath, she backed out of his arms and pointed to it on the small table by her bed. "And get the locked box out of the drawer underneath it."

"What's in it?" He grinned at her. "Condoms?"

Abby rolled her eyes. "Something even better for protection—my backup gun and ammo."

Hawk looked impressed. "A woman after my own heart."

He headed for the nightstand while she did her best to get her racing pulse back under control—but *whew*. The guy's kiss packed a punch. Past him, on the floor, she could see the clothes she'd tried on yesterday and discarded, and then tried on again before deciding what to wear to a raid with the man she'd been secretly lusting over, as if it had been a date. Which was a joke, because she hadn't dated since...

Since Gaines. And their last date hadn't exactly been a rousing success—

Oh, God.

It all came back to her. He'd taken her to his second home, a luxurious ranch outside of Cheyenne, a "secret haven" he'd called it.

Secret haven.

"Abby?" Hawk put his hands on her arm. "What is it?"

What was it? Suddenly, she knew where to find Gaines.

19

Cheyenne Memorial Hospital

LOGAN OPENED HIS EYES WITH some trepidation, but to his relief the blazing pain in his head had faded to a dull throbbing.

He could live with that.

Another thing he could live with? The woman curled up at his side.

Callen had stayed. Well, mostly because she hadn't wanted him to leave the hospital, but he knew it was more than that. Any woman who held his head while he tossed his cookies on a helicopter, risked her job to hide him, then played strip poker just to make him listen to her, was interested in more than just a patient/nurse relationship.

Or so he hoped. He stroked a hand down her side and she jerked straight up, eyes clear. "You hurting?" she asked.

"Yes."

Leaning in, frown in place, she put a hand to his forehead, but he took it in his and brought it to his chest.

There. That felt slightly better. But he wanted to pull her entirely inside him. "Here. I hurt here."

Still frowning, she yanked his hospital gown down to stare at his chest, her fingers running softly over his skin. "I don't see anything. Let me call the doctor—"

"No, it's not that kind of injury. Listen, Hawk's going to call—"

"He already did. He's coming for you. But—"

"No buts. We won't have time for this once he gets here, and before I go—"

"If you're in pain, we should rethink you going at all."

"Before I go," he repeated, "and make a really big fool out of myself here, I just want to ask you something. About last night." He met her gaze. "It was different, right? I mean, for you, too—"

"I've never been with a patient like this before, if that's what you're asking." Callen looked down at their clasped hands. "Never. In fact, I haven't…with anyone…in a long time. I haven't met anyone that I wanted— I've been working a lot, and—" She bit her lip and shook her head. "No, those are lies. A year ago I got out of a long relationship, and I haven't wanted to risk my heart again."

"Makes perfect sense, since I feel the same way. Or did, until about twelve hours ago."

"Logan—"

"Look, I know this is ridiculously fast, but I've just got to tell you, before today goes straight to hell—"

"No. No going straight to hell. No going anywhere."

"Actually, yes, I am. With Hawk, but—" He blinked, as he realized something. "I'm not in the same room as before."

"No."

His old room had been white, stark and smelled sterile. This one had soft pastel painted walls and different equipment—very different. Stirrups, for one. *Huh.* "Where am I, Callen?"

"I moved you. You're under a different name, on a different floor. Hawk's idea."

Good. It didn't matter where he was, as long as he got out to help Hawk. "I'll need clothes."

"Logan, this is crazy. *You're* crazy."

"Crazy. Yes. Crazy for you. You should know, I have no idea where this thing is going between us. I only know that I don't want it to end when I leave here."

"Oh." She breathed this softly, with no hint of whether that was a good or bad *oh*. So he swallowed hard and did the only thing he could, which was lay it all out for her.

"I want to see you again after this is over."

"You want to see me again."

"Tonight, if possible."

"Tonight."

"And tomorrow. And the next day. And—"

"I…get the idea."

"But do you like the idea?"

Her smile warmed his heart. "Okay, but Logan? I'm coming with you—"

"No. No way."

"You'll need a nurse. Especially one with access

to stimulants that can keep you on your feet long enough to get somewhere safe, and take care of you when you collapse after they wear off."

"No, Callen. I'm not risking you."

She let it go while she brought him clothes. And when he saw what she brought him, he shook his head. "*Hell*, no."

"If the entrances and exits are being watched…" She smiled cajolingly. "A brand new momma is the perfect disguise to get you out of here undetected."

Logan stared at the huge tent dress, wig and bag of makeup. "Fuck me."

She grinned. "Ah, honey. Maybe later. But for now, let's pimp you up." She helped him pull the huge dress over his head, fussing with it, then standing back to admire it.

He shook his head. "You're enjoying this way too much."

"Uh-huh." She placed a dark blond frizzy wig on his head that made him look like a white RuPaul. "Cherry or strawberry?" she asked.

"Huh?"

"Lip gloss."

"Uh—"

"Strawberry," she decided, and stepped between his legs to apply the makeup.

His hands went to her hips and he pulled her in snugly, or as snug as she could get with his cast up to his thigh. It wasn't close enough. He spread his legs wider and let his hand slide down her back to squeeze her ass.

"Well." Callen laughed. "I've never been come on to by a woman before."

"It's different for me, too, believe me." He let his hand slip into her scrubs, then beneath the edging of her panties.

Her breath caught. "It feels kinky."

He'd like to show her a whole bunch more kink but not in a damn dress, that was for sure.

Then she brought him a mirror and he stared at the female version of himself.

He was the ugliest woman he'd ever seen. "I can't believe you let me touch you."

She snorted, then pulled out a wheelchair.

"Uh-uh. I don't need—"

She shoved a wrapped bundle into his arms. He stared down at the fake baby. "Okay, this is weird."

"What, the clothing?"

"No. The baby. I've never really seen myself with kids."

"Never?" She crouched to add booties over his very male feet.

"I guess I never figured myself as the kind of guy who'd settle down and have a woman love him enough to give him a kid."

Callen glanced up into his face, her hand on his thigh. "You know what that means, right?"

"No, what?"

"That you've never been with the right woman."

He stared into her eyes, and suddenly found his throat tight. "Is that right?"

Gaze latched on his, she slowly nodded.

"So would you have any idea where I'd find the right woman?"

Her eyes went suspiciously shiny, but she only smiled.

Abby's condo complex

"I THINK I KNOW WHERE Gaines is," Abby told Hawk. "He's got another piece of property he doesn't tell people about, an upscale ranch house about thirty minutes from here."

Hawk absorbed this as they quickly moved back through the gate and along the path, her laptop tucked beneath his arm, her gun in his waistband. He kept one hand free as they headed to the SUV, watching all the angles, his expression dangerous.

She couldn't take her eyes off him. Somehow she'd been caught up in this perilous game between two men capable of doing whatever they needed done. Just days ago she'd have said she didn't trust either of them fully.

But she couldn't say that now. Scary as Hawk seemed as he led her back to the relative safety of the SUV, she knew the truth.

She trusted him with her life. "Hawk."

He opened the driver's side and urged her in. "Yeah?"

She waited until he'd pulled out of the parking lot. "Do you remember the first thing I said to you last night?"

He sped down the road. "The part about you trusting a rat's ass before you could trust me?"

"Um, yeah." She winced. "That." They'd both been Gaines's victims. But no longer. "I've changed my mind."

He glanced at her with an arched eyebrow. She'd surprised him.

"I can trust you. With anything."

"Hold that thought," he said, and whipped them onto a side construction road so fast her hand slapped on the dash. He steered them behind a cluster of trees and yanked on the brake.

"What are you doing?"

"This." Hauling her to him, he covered her mouth with his.

Yeah, this. This was what she needed. She sank into the kiss, wrapping her arms around him, running her hands up and down his back, over his shoulders, up his neck into his hair, everywhere she could reach. She couldn't get enough of touching him. In this spinning, out-of-control world, he'd become her anchor, her rock.

And given the way he clutched at her, his own hands fighting with hers for purchase, skimming up her sides, her spine, then back to the front, beneath her shirt now, skin to skin, he felt the same way. "I don't want anything to happen to you." His lips brushed her skin.

"It won't." She cupped his face as he gently set his forehead to hers. They stayed that way a moment before Hawk drew a deep breath and lifted his head to look into her eyes.

He'd shifted gears already, and she took a moment to catch up.

"Abby."

She sighed.

"Gaines's ranch. Can you tell me where it is?"

"That would be a really bad idea."

"Or a really good one."

She understood the problem. Without ever wanting to, she'd become his soft spot, his Achilles' heel. Whether she was with him by choice or not didn't matter to Gaines, that she was with him at all made her a problem. A dispensable one. If he didn't get to Gaines, Gaines would likely get to him. And her. "I can draw you a map," she admitted.

"Good." Hawk punched some numbers into her cell phone. "Callen? Is he ready?" He listened, and his brow raised as he glanced at Abby. "I can talk to him? Great, thanks." There was a pause. "God, Logan, are you ever a sound for sore ears—"

His voice was so husky with emotion, she felt her throat tighten.

"Are you sure you're up for this, Logan, because—yeah, I hear you. Jesus, am I glad to hear you."

Abby looked out the window, concentrating on breathing as she listened to their reunion. They spoke in short, clipped sentences that spoke of the long-time ease between them, and an ability to guess what the other was thinking.

She'd never had a relationship like that in her entire life, because she didn't open up. She had started to with Gaines, and look what had happened. He'd set her up to be tortured.

How was she supposed to ever trust her judgment again?

She peeked at Hawk, still talking to Logan. He was trying to line up a secure place to dump her. Was she going to let him do that?

"I want her safe."

The words did something to the cold spot in her heart. The truth was, in spite of herself, she *had* learned to trust again. She knew Hawk was innocent. She knew he cared about her, and the knowledge warmed her in a way she'd never experienced.

She wished they were still at the B&B and she was back in his arms, where everything was okay as long as he kept holding her. Because with him, no matter what was going on, she felt safe. "Hawk, I'm staying with you."

Eyeing her, he said into the phone, "Are you sure, because Christ, Logan—yeah. Okay. We'll be right there to get you. Yeah, 'we.'" With a sigh, he closed the phone and reached behind him for her laptop, which he handed to her. "Serial numbers."

"What's the matter?"

He shook his head. "In a minute. Look up the serial numbers."

She started up her computer and her e-mail program automatically opened. On a hunch, Abby opened some old files, then leaned back and shook her head.

"What?" Hawk leaned over her to try and see.

"You said you shot Gaines on that raid eighteen months ago."

"Yes."

"You didn't know it was Gaines at the time."

"I didn't come to suspect so until later, no."

"Eighteen months ago he took a one-month leave." She flipped through several e-mails from him from that time. "Emergency appendicitis." She looked at him. "Too bad I don't believe in coincidence." Feeling overwhelmed by how big this was, she rubbed her hands over her face. "My God."

He reached for her, but she straightened and shook her head. Not the time to fall apart. "The serial numbers." While she pulled up another file, he grabbed the confiscated rifle and read her the number.

Abby's stomach thumped as she matched it to her list. "It's here. Now tell me what Logan said to put that look on your face."

"Tibbs called again. They know the body wasn't Gaines."

Their eyes met. "Then who?"

"Watkins."

"Oh, my God." So Gaines had killed one of his own. Knowing it rammed home another certainty— Gaines would stop at nothing to get what he wanted.

"Gaines had Logan pushed off that roof to kill him," Hawk told her. "He needs us dead."

"Which is a very good reason *not* to go to his ranch."

"Or *to* go." There was knowledge in his eyes and acceptance.

Oh, God. He was going there to end this, one way or another, for her. So she'd be safe. "Hawk," she said. "You are not going to go there to die."

"Not me, no."

He sat there, so serious, so determined, she felt her heart just give in. From the very beginning he'd evoked myriad emotions from her—annoyance, lust, more annoyance, awe, affection, the ever-popular annoyance...and now, love. "We need to go to Tibbs."

Hawk let out a low laugh. "So he can hold me while they sort this out?"

"He won't—"

"He would, yes. That's his job. We'll call him, but when it's too late to stop me from finishing this with Gaines." His eyes were hard, his voice tight. "Which we do today."

20

Cheyenne Memorial Hospital

HAWK AND ABBY PULLED INTO the hospital parking lot just as a nurse wheeled out a large woman and her baby.

Hawk hopped out of the SUV, squatted before the wheelchair and grinned for the first time in two days. "Congratulations on your new arrival."

"Fuck you," Logan said from beneath his Vegas showgirl–style wig. He looked at Abby, then back at Hawk. "Huh?"

"What?"

"I just never thought you'd ever land yourself someone as classy as Abby, that's all."

Abby's brow shot up. "And how do you know he 'landed' me?"

"It's all over your face. Both your faces."

She blinked, then looked at the pretty nurse behind Logan, who smiled and held out her hand. "Hi, I'm Callen. And don't worry, I don't see anything but a lovely glow."

Abby put her hands to her face. Hawk looked

over Logan's multitude of injuries, then glanced at Callen. "You didn't do so shabby either."

Logan reached for Callen's hand. "Yeah, I did pretty darn great."

Callen smiled dreamily, but that faded as two police cars pulled into the lot. "I wonder if that's related to our new problem?"

"New problem?" Hawk asked.

"Later. Run now." They all piled into the vehicle, with Logan looking a little green despite his grin, which told Hawk he was hurting much more than he wanted to let on.

"New problem?" Hawk demanded from behind the wheel. "And the cops? What do they want? My head?"

"On a platter," Logan said. "The ATF has large sums of money going in and out of your accounts. *Out* being the key operative here, apparently. Supposedly you've just withdrawn a huge sum of money. Then there's the memory stick Tibbs found. And, wait for it…in spite of the fact that they do not have Gaines's body and all the evidence is looking right at *him*, they're charging *you* with kidnapping Abby."

"Is that all?" Hawk asked in tune to Abby's gasp. "Hell, that's not too bad." He met Logan's gaze in the rearview mirror. "We'll go to Gaines's ranch in two hours."

"Why two hours?"

"Because nightfall will be a better time to get close to Gaines."

"We can go to my place," Callen said.

It seemed as good a plan as any, especially since

Logan really did look like death warmed over and Abby seemed ready to shatter. They'd take a few minutes, hopefully get their game plan together and finish this.

One way or another.

Callen's condo

HAWK PACED CALLEN'S SMALL spare bedroom while Abby sat on the bed watching him. "Okay," he said. "So he's got the money, freshly laundered through my account. He's going to vanish, and soon. Unfortunately, he's run into a snag. Me."

"If he sees you, you're dead."

"Right," he agreed. "Which is option number one."

"And option number two is?"

She sounded pissed, a front for her fear, which he appreciated, but he didn't plan on dying. "Me turning myself in on the mercy of the legal system."

Abby's eyes were conflicted. "I've been thinking about that. Given how he's handled everything so ruthlessly, that's not a good option. He'll try to have you killed while you're waiting for justice."

"Probably."

"So we move to option three," Abby said tightly. "Which is me offering myself up."

He stared at her in utter speechlessness. Finally, he managed to say, "Over my dead body."

"No, listen. We both know he has this obsession with me. He's got an ego the size of Texas, right?

And he thinks I worship the ground he walks on, that's what keeps that ego going. You know it," she continued when he opened his mouth. "I'm the one thing he never got, and it's eating at him, Hawk, you know it is. I offer to go with him if he leaves you alone. It might work."

"Abby." His belly felt hollow. That she'd even suggested it after what she'd been through last year told him how much he meant to her. Touched beyond words, he ran a finger over the cut on her cheek, then leaned in and kissed it. "Not happening."

"I don't want you to die."

"Makes two of us."

She looked into his eyes, her own soft and sweet and heartbreakingly open. "Remember last night, when you said you'd do anything to make this all up to me?"

"Of course."

She backed to the door and hit the lock.

"What are you doing?"

Her hands came up and pulled off Serena's sweater, beneath which she wore her own bra. "I just figured out how you can do that."

"Oh, yeah?" Hawk's voice was no longer so steady, and neither were his hands as he shoved them in his pockets to try to keep them off her. But God, she stood there, offering him everything with her eyes, her body….

She reached for the zipper on the jeans. It was a tribute to how much she'd stunned him that she managed to shimmy out of them before he moved.

Good Christ, she *was* commando. "Abby—" He reached for her but she slapped a hand to his chest.

"No, I'm not naked yet. I want to be naked with you."

His mouth went dry. All of his blood rushed to his groin so fast he got dizzy.

"Please, Hawk," she murmured, unhooking her bra and letting it drop, standing before him, gloriously nude. "Love me."

The kicker? He already did. So goddamn much he could hardly breathe. Gently pulling her in against him, he slowly backed her to the bed, following her down, down...ah, yeah, ending up right where he wanted to be, between her legs.

Home.

Her lips were soft, receptive and made for his, and kissing her was like heaven on earth. So was touching her. Never in a million years had he expected her to offer this again, to want him in the way he wanted her, and it hit like a freight train. "Abby."

She was busy, her mouth spreading hot, sweet kisses down his throat, her hands shoving his jeans down at the same time so that she could wrap a leg around him, opening herself up so he could sink inside her.

God.

Yeah, he might have spent six months fantasizing about her, but those dreams had nothing, nothing at all, on the reality of being with her, feeling her body move with his, hearing her pant out his name as if there was no one else on earth who could do her right. The only sound in the room now was their

harsh breathing as they struggled to keep their wordless pleas and moans from being overheard. Being
with her like this was beyond his dreams, so sensual,
so earthy and erotic as hell. It was also oddly unnerving because he knew…

She was it for him.

Her breasts were cushioned against his chest, her
belly to his, her body soft against his hard, ungiving
one. He had his hands on her ass, with each thrust
driving them higher and higher, and he looked into
her face, watching her go over for him, shatter with
his name on her lips. Lost in her shudders, so sweetly
encased in her body, he came right along with her,
with only one thought in his brain.

Oh, yeah, he'd fallen. He'd fallen good and hard,
and couldn't get up.

THE PLAN WAS SIMPLE, BUT STILL struck terror into
Abby's heart. She'd described the lay of the ranch
for Hawk and Logan. They'd wait until they were
nearly there to call Tibbs and give him directions.
That way he would be too late to stop them, but not
too late to help.

Hopefully.

The possibility made Abby sick to her stomach.
So many things could go wrong. Gaines could kill
Logan and Hawk or her before admitting anything.
Tibbs could not show up in time, or worse, show up
too soon and take Hawk into custody.

The whole thing was one big crap shoot, and
Abby hated gambling.

Logan, changed out of his maternal wear, got into the passenger seat of the SUV, looking far too weak for Abby's peace of mind, but there was no stopping this. He leaned out the window and gave Callen a kiss good-bye. "I'll never forget you," he said more solemnly than Abby had ever seen him.

Callen shook her head, eyes fierce. "Oh, no. Hell, no. Don't you dare say good-bye to me like you're not coming back."

Logan didn't smile, or try to reassure her. "Callen—"

"You know what? Forget this bullshit." And she climbed into the backseat. "I'm in as much danger if I stay behind. I gave Gaines my name when I thought he was your boss, and by now they've probably noticed you disappeared just before I left the hospital."

Hawk looked at Abby. "This is crazy."

Callen lifted a small tape recorder. "Not crazy. I can help. Hey, I might get something useful for you all to use later, right?"

"Absolutely crazy," Hawk repeated.

"There's no doubt of that." Abby gestured to the wheel. "You driving, or am I?"

"Shit." But he opened the backseat for her, and then got behind the wheel.

The plan was in motion now, and nothing could stop it. Abby met Hawk's gaze in the mirror and realized one thing she'd forgotten to do, one thing that was going to haunt her if things went bad.

She'd forgotten to tell him she loved him.

GAINES'S RANCH WAS HIGH IN the hills, in rough terrain, and extremely remote. Hawk didn't take the turn into its long dirt driveway. Instead, he took them on a four-wheel tour through the woods, entering onto the property from the back.

At the edge of a clearing, he stopped the vehicle. Down a ravine, about a half mile ahead, sat the ranch house, completely isolated. It was surrounded on two sides by running streams, and a third side by a rocky, sheer cliff.

Terrific.

"We're going to have to hike in," he told Logan.

They all looked at Logan's cast.

"No problem," Logan said confidently, and lifted his cane. "I'm feeling no pain."

Hawk doubted that but he knew he couldn't keep Logan from going—he'd follow him anyway. Abby was another story. He got out of the car and stopped her from doing the same. Leaning in, he put his hands on her face just to touch her, waiting until she slayed him with those eyes. "Someone needs to stay behind and protect Callen. I'll leave you the rifle. If we don't come back, get behind the wheel and drive the hell out of here."

"Hawk—"

"Go directly to Regional. Plant yourself there to protect yourself from Gaines's revenge, tell Tibbs I kidnapped you against your will, if necessary—"

"I am not going to put that nail in your coffin—"

"Abby, listen to me. If I don't come back, you won't need the nails. Show him your cuts, your bruises, the rifle, okay? Go back to Selena's and get my cuffs. The truck. With all the evidence they'll believe you."

Her eyes filled. "If you don't get out of that ranch house, I'll kill you myself."

He smiled, though he knew his eyes were shiny, too. "That's a deal." Hawk smoothed back her hair, and kissed her once because he couldn't resist, letting their lips cling for a beat. "See you on the other side, Ab." He wanted to drop to his knees, take her hand and ask her to love him forever. Yeah, he really wanted to do that. But he had to survive the next hour before he asked her for her heart and soul, that seemed only fair. So he turned, and with Logan, walked away.

But he left his heart with her.

FIFTEEN SWEATY MINUTES LATER, Hawk and Logan came to one of the streams.

"Oh, boy." Logan weaved unsteadily.

Hawk reached out to grab him. "You okay?"

"Ask him."

Hawk followed Logan's gaze to a big-ass moose, who stood twenty-five yards away, watching them balefully. Between his huge palmated antlers, his elongated snout wriggled as he took in their scent.

"Just keep moving," Hawk said. "I've got your back."

"Why do I have to go first?"

"Because you're the injured one. The one most likely to get eaten. Jesus. Just go!"

The moose wriggled his nose again but was too lazy

to chase them. It took another fifteen minutes to get down to Gaines's house. Gaines's deserted ranch house.

"Think the bastard already took off?" Not looking so hot, Logan sank to the porch swing.

"No." But it was so still as to be eerie. "He's here, somewhere."

Any minute, Tibbs and company were going to burst in with a blaze of glory, and damn it, having Gaines here would be ever so helpful. Hawk stepped into the yard and turned in a slow circle. "He's probably watching us."

"If that was true, we'd already be dead."

"Then he's watching something else." Narrowing his gaze, he turned again, stopping short at the sight of a surveillance camera mounted in the tree off the right side of the porch. A matching camera was on the left. And he'd bet every last cent he had, there were many, many more. *Shit.* He whipped back to Logan. "Abby and Callen."

"What?"

"This place is surrounded by cameras. He's been onto us since we first arrived. He's probably already at the car."

Logan swore and got to his feet, huffing and puffing. "Jesus. I'm worthless. The drugs are wearing off. Just go."

Hawk came back to him and shoved a shoulder into one of Logan's armpits, working as a human crutch. "Like I'm going to leave you behind now, after all these years that I've been carting your sorry ass around."

"Shut up and run."

It felt like it took them an eternity, but in twelve minutes they were back at the top of the hill, where they separated to circle around. Hawk came in from the east and hugged up to a tree. Damn it, he couldn't see. He'd have to climb the tree, which led him twenty feet straight up into hell before he had a good, dizzying, oh-holy-shit view.

God, he hated heights. But he hated what he saw even more. In front of the SUV, Callen was crumpled on the ground, eyes closed.

And Gaines. The bastard was leaning back against the car as if he had all the time in the world, Abby held tight to him, a gun to her temple.

"Might as well come out and join the party," Gaines called out.

Bullshit. Hawk aimed his gun directly between Gaines's eyes, which unfortunately put him damn close to between Abby's as well. "Let her go."

At the sound of his voice, Abby gasped and looked up until she locked gazes with him. "I'm sorry," she said. "He got the jump on me."

"Of course I found you." Gaines pressed his cheek to hers. "I always will. Now, here's how this is going to work, Hawk. You're going to put down your gun. And Logan? I know you're out there. Might as well show yourself."

Logan did not appear. Hawk had no idea if this was strategy, or if he hadn't made it around yet. "Let

her go," he repeated, his gun still sighted right between Gaines's bloodshot eyes. "Do it. Or I promise you, this will hurt."

"I'm sorry." And actually, Gaines did look sorry. He
sported a bandage around his shoulder that reminded
Hawk he'd shot the bastard last night. "I can't always
be looking for you over my shoulder. You have to die."

"No," Abby gasped, terror filling her gaze, terror
for Hawk. "Elliot, don't be stupid, you'll never get
away with this."

"You'd be surprised what I can get away with."
Again, he ran his cheek over hers, his eyes softening. Then he shifted the muzzle of his gun from her
temple to just beneath her jaw, and Hawk's heart
just about stopped. The guy's hands were shaking,
he was a loose cannon who was going to go off and
shoot her in the process.

No. He wasn't going to let that happen. If he could
get Abby to go limp and drop, he could get a clean
shot. "Do you remember that one thing I wanted
from you?" he asked.

She nodded. Trust. It was there in her eyes for him
to accept, take. "Good," he told her, and nodded his
head once, trying to signal her to drop. "That's real
good." As his finger applied slow pressure, she
looked him right in the eyes and mouthed "I love
you," and on that stunning revelation, she didn't drop
but shoved back with her elbow, landing it hard in
Gaines's windpipe. A harsh sound expelled from his
lungs, and then Abby dropped, in that split second
giving Hawk the free target he needed.

Except that before he got a shot off, a different gun rang out, and both Gaines and Abby crumpled to the ground.

Hawk slid down the tree, racing toward the pair as Logan burst out of the woods, limping toward them, his gun in hand.

Hawk had never been so petrified in his life as he was in that very moment, that single moment of clarity, when he knew he was never going to be the same. Abby had just come into his life. With her smile, with every breath she took, she'd made it better.

She'd made him whole.

Goddamn, but he'd been waiting for that without even knowing it, and now that he'd experienced it, he was afraid he couldn't live without it.

Without her.

_21_

BEFORE ABBY COULD DRAW A breath into her compressed lungs, the heavy weight was lifted off of her, and she was yanked into a pair of strong, warm arms.

Trembling arms.

"Jesus, Abby." Hawk pulled back only enough to look down into her face.

"Hey," she told him. "Good shot."

"It wasn't me, it was Logan." He gulped for air. "Tell me you did not just say you love me when I had a gun pointed at your head."

She smiled as her eyes filled. She couldn't help it. "I did."

His eyes went misty, and he hauled her back into his arms.

She let him squeeze the air out of her because that was where she needed to be, in his arms, tight, face plastered into the crook of his neck, inhaling his scent, feeling as if she'd just come home for the first time in her life. They might have both been victims, but no longer. They had survived, because they were stronger together. "Is Gaines—"

"I don't know." He palmed her head in his hands and held her face to his throat. "Are you—"

"Fine," she promised. "Callen—"

"Logan's got her, she's coming around." They both turned.

Logan was holding onto Callen the same way Hawk was holding onto Abby, but Callen was shaking her head. "I'm fine, he got me from behind, knocked me out cold, but I'm good now." She managed to pull the tape recorder out from beneath her shirt. "Like me and the Energizer Bunny, this kept going."

From behind the SUV, Tibbs, Thomas and Wayne appeared, running.

"About time," Hawk said.

Tibbs held out his hand for the recorder. "Can I see that?"

Callen handed it over, and Tibbs tucked it away, nodding to first Logan, and then to Hawk, who visibly tensed.

But Tibbs didn't shoot him, didn't handcuff him, didn't do anything but let out a slow nod of approval. "Should have trusted me, Hawk. I'm not stupid enough to believe you'd leave incriminating evidence lying around your house. Luckily I was only half a step behind you."

Thomas and Wayne crouched at Gaines's side and turned him over. "Still breathing," Thomas noted.

Wayne radioed for the ambulance. "He's not going to thank us."

Logan hadn't taken his eyes off Callen. "He could have killed you. I'll never forgive myself for—"

"But he didn't kill me. And you're still alive, too,"

she pointed out. "So now that no one's dying today, maybe we can make plans, and do things right."

Logan looked shaken to the core, and as if he'd been hit by a bus. In a good way. "You mean we didn't do things right before?"

Callen smiled. "Well, you not being hooked up to any machines will be a bonus."

"True." He snagged her close, pulled her into his lap and just sat there. "Except I'm too tired to move."

"Don't worry. I have enough energy to keep us both moving."

Hawk tipped his head down to Abby, not looking nearly as ready to joke as Logan and Callen.

"You climbed a tree for me," Abby marveled. "A really tall pine tree."

"Thanks for noticing." He ran a hand down her hair, cupping her jaw. He couldn't stop looking at her.

"I'm really okay you know."

"Good." He sank all the way to the ground, holding her tight to him. "That's good, because I'm not."

"What? Did you get hurt?" Panicked, she ran her hands over his chest, his face, his arms, until he caught them in his.

"No, listen. I love you back, Abby. So much I don't even know what to do with it all."

She stared up into the face of the man she'd given herself over to so completely. "Really?"

"God, yes."

She felt so much joy she could hardly breathe. "Well, I have some ideas on what to do with it."

"I knew you would," he said fiercely, and beneath the setting sun, he kissed her to show that maybe he had a few ideas of his own.

Epilogue

Two weeks later

ABBY CLOSED HER CELL PHONE and smiled. She also purred and stretched like a kitten because there was a pair of big, strong hands spreading suntan lotion on her back, smoothing it up and down in a delicious motion as she lay sprawled out in a large, comfy beach chair beneath a palm tree, the gorgeous crystal-clear ocean hitting the shore only five feet in front of her.... "Mmm."

The South Pacific was definitely all it was cracked up to be.

The fingers dug in a little, loosening up her muscles, and she let out a heartfelt appreciative moan. Then a mouth skimmed her ear.

"What did Tibbs want?" that mouth asked, her own personal cabana boy. God, she loved it when he sounded like that, all low and sexy. She flipped over and smiled up at Hawk, who was pouring more lotion in his hands.

Her body tingled in anticipation.

Since she wore only bikini bottoms, he could see

exactly what he did to her. His gaze settled on her bare breasts, watching her nipples harden, and he let out a slow smile that had other reactions going on in her as well. She knew that heavy lidded look, knew what it meant.

Then he settled his hands on her belly and began smoothing in the lotion. Wearing only a pair of board shorts low on his hips, his hard body bronzed from two weeks in the sun, he could have passed for one of the natives here on this South Pacific island.

"Abby?"

Right. He'd asked her a question. "He wanted to make sure we're enjoying our entire forced leave—" She broke off when his hands began their ascent, heading up her ribs…

"It's tough, of course," he said. "The forced leave. But someone's got to do it."

They grinned at each other, and Hawk's hands continued to glide up her torso to her breasts. They were on their own private little beach, with their own private little luxurious hut behind them, only a quarter of a mile away from Logan's and Callen's equally private hut. Tibbs had given the four of them the trip that Gaines himself had planned to take, in reward for their service to the ATF. They'd been ordered to spend the time recouping, recovering and relaxing.

Abby was doing all three, with flying colors. "He also wanted to remind us that we still have two weeks left and he doesn't want to see us early. But that when he does, there's going to be a little change. We're getting raises."

"I like that part."

"Me, too."

"But I have a change of my own."

Hawk's thumbs slowly circled her nipples, and her breath caught. "Ch-change?"

"Of status." Nudging her to scoot over, he slid onto the lounger and pulled her close.

She shifted so that one of his thighs was between hers but when he cupped her face, looking so serious, her heart skipped a beat.

"I love you," he said solemnly, fiercely.

Ah. She was never going to get tired of hearing that. "I love you back, Hawk. So much."

"My own miracle…" He stroked a strand of hair from her face. "I know this might seem fast to you, but I've been finding myself feeling…well, old-fashioned and proprietary."

"Old-fashioned? Proprietary?" Abby looked down at her bare breasts, which were plumped up against his chest. "Meaning what, we have to stop getting naked?"

"Meaning I want to marry you. And live happily ever after."

She blinked as a warmth spread outward from the very depths of her soul.

"So…what do you think?"

"That I could get used to old-fashioned and proprietary."

Hawk let out a breath and pressed his forehead to hers. "Abby."

Cupping his face, she pulled back to see into his eyes. "Just thought of something. Old-fashioned…

does that mean we can't sleep together before we make it legal?"

A slow, wicked grin pulled at his mouth, and he slid a hand down her spine and into her bikini bottoms, his fingers dipping low enough to make her shiver. "If I said yes, would you—"

"I'd find a way to get married right here and now," she declared unevenly as he stripped off her bottoms and his fingers got very, very busy.

"You know…" Lowering his head, he began to kiss his way down her neck. "Did I ever tell you that Logan is an ordained minister? He did it online several years ago as a joke."

"I love Logan."

"But you love me more."

Abby arched back as Hawk rolled, tucking her beneath him, gasping when he slid into her. "I love you more," she agreed. "I love you for always…."

* * * * *

THE ROYAL HOUSE OF NIROLI
Always passionate, always proud

The richest royal family in the world—united by blood and passion, torn apart by deceit and desire.

Nestled in the azure blue of the Mediterranean Sea, the majestic island of Niroli has prospered for centuries. The Fierezza men have worn the crown with passion and pride since ancient times. But now, as the king's health declines, and his two sons have been tragically killed, the crown is in jeopardy.

The clock is ticking—a new heir must be found before the king is forced to abdicate. By royal decree the internationally scattered members of the Fierezza family are summoned to claim their destiny. But any person who takes the throne must do so according to The Rules of the Royal House of Niroli. Soon secrets and rivalries emerge as the descendents of this ancient royal line vie for position and power. Only a true Fierezza can become ruler—a person dedicated to their country, their people…and their eternal love!

Each month starting in July 2007,
Harlequin Presents is delighted to bring you
an exciting installment from
THE ROYAL HOUSE OF NIROLI,
in which you can follow the epic search
for the true Nirolian king.
Eight heirs, eight romances, eight fantastic stories!
Here's your chance to enjoy a sneak preview of the first book delivered to you by royal decree….

FIVE MINUTES later she was standing immobile in front of the study's window, her original purpose of coming in forgotten, as she stared in shocked horror at the envelope she was holding. Waves of heat followed by icy chills surged through her body. She could hardly see the address now through her blurred vision, but the crest on its left-hand front corner stood out, its *royal* crest, followed by the address: *HRH Prince Marco of Niroli...*

She didn't hear Marco's key in the apartment door, she didn't even hear him calling out her name. Her shock was so great that nothing could penetrate it. It encased her in a kind of bubble, which only concentrated the torment of what she was suffering and branded it on her brain so that it could never be forgotten. It was only finally pierced by the sudden opening of the study door as Marco walked in.

"Welcome home, *Your Highness*. I suppose I ought to curtsy." She waited, praying that he would laugh and tell her that she had got it all wrong, that the envelope she was holding, addressing him as Prince Marco of Niroli, was some silly mistake. But like a tiny candle flame shivering vulnerably in the dark, her hope trembled fearfully. And then the look in Marco's eyes extinguished it as cruelly as a hand placed callously over a dying person's face to stem their last breath.

"Give that to me," he demanded, taking the envelope from her.

"It's too late, Marco," Emily told him brokenly. "I know the truth now…." She dug her teeth in her lower lip to try to force back her own pain.

"You had no right to go through my desk," Marco shot back at her furiously, full of loathing at being caught off-guard and forced into a position in which he was in the wrong, making him determined to find something he could accuse Emily of. "I trusted you…."

Emily could hardly believe what she was hearing. "No, you didn't trust me, Marco, and you didn't trust me because you knew that I couldn't trust you. And you knew that because you're a liar, and liars don't trust people because they know that they themselves cannot be trusted." She not only felt sick, she also felt as though she could hardly breathe. "You are Prince Marco of Niroli…. How could you not tell me who you are and still live with me as intimately as we have lived together?" she demanded brokenly.

"Stop being so ridiculously dramatic," Marco demanded fiercely. "You are making too much of the situation."

"*Too much?*" Emily almost screamed the words at him. "When were you going to tell me, Marco?

Perhaps you just planned to walk away without telling me anything? After all, what do my feelings matter to you?"

"Of course they matter." Marco stopped her sharply. "And it was in part to protect them, and you, that I decided not to inform you when my grandfather first announced that he intended to step down from the throne and hand it on to me."

"To protect me?" Emily nearly choked on her fury. "Hand on the throne? No wonder you told me when you first took me to bed that all you wanted was sex. You *knew* that was the only kind of relationship there could ever be between us! You *knew* that one day you would be Niroli's king. No doubt you are expected to marry a princess. Is she picked out for you already, your *royal* bride?"

* * * * *

Look for THE FUTURE KING'S PREGNANT MISTRESS
by Penny Jordan in July 2007,
from Harlequin Presents,
available wherever books are sold.

HARLEQUIN®

Mediterranean NIGHTS™

Experience the glamour and elegance of cruising the high seas with a new 12-book series....

MEDITERRANEAN NIGHTS

Coming in July 2007...

SCENT OF A WOMAN

by

Joanne Rock

When Danielle Chevalier is invited to an exclusive conference aboard *Alexandra's Dream,* she knows it will mean good things for her struggling fragrance company. But her dreams get a setback when she meets Adam Burns, a representative from a large American conglomerate.

Danielle is charmed by the brusque American— until she finds out he means to compete with her bid for the opportunity that will save her family business!

Romantic
SUSPENSE

Sparked by Danger, Fueled by Passion.

Mission: Impassioned

A brand-new miniseries begins with

My Spy

By *USA TODAY* bestselling author

Marie Ferrarella

She had to trust him with her life....
It was the most daring mission of Joshua Lazlo's
career: rescuing the prime minister of England's
daughter from a gang of cold-blooded kidnappers.
But nothing prepared the shadowy secret agent
for a fiery woman whose touch ignited something
far more dangerous.

My Spy

#1472

Available July 2007 wherever you buy books!

REQUEST YOUR FREE BOOKS!

2 FREE NOVELS PLUS 2 FREE GIFTS!

HARLEQUIN®

Blaze

Red-hot reads!

HB07

Do you know
a real-life heroine?

Nominate her for the Harlequin
More Than Words award.

Each year Harlequin Enterprises honors five
ordinary women for their extraordinary
commitment to their community.

Each recipient of the Harlequin More Than Words
award receives a $10,000 donation from Harlequin
to advance the work of her chosen charity. And five
of Harlequin's most acclaimed authors donate their
time and creative talents to writing a novella inspired
by the award recipients. The More Than Words
anthology is published annually in October and all
proceeds benefit causes of concern to women.

HARLEQUIN

More Than Words™

**For more details or to nominate
a woman you know please visit**

www.HarlequinMoreThanWords.com

MTW2007

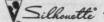

SPECIAL EDITION™

Look for six new
MONTANA MAVERICKS
stories, beginning in July with

THE MAN WHO HAD EVERYTHING

by *CHRISTINE RIMMER*

When Grant Clifton decided to sell the family ranch, he knew it would devastate Stephanie Julen, the caretaker who'd always been like a little sister to him. He wanted a new start, but how could he tell her that she and her mother would have to leave...especially now that he was head over heels in love with her?

MONTANA MAVERICKS

Dreaming big—and winning hearts—in Big Sky Country

Silhouette Desire

THE GARRISONS
A brand-new family saga begins with

THE CEO'S SCANDALOUS AFFAIR
BY ROXANNE ST. CLAIRE

Eldest son Parker Garrison is preoccupied running
his Miami hotel empire and dealing with his recently
deceased father's secret second family. Since he has
little time to date, taking his superefficient assistant
to a charity event should have been a simple plan.
Until passion takes them beyond business.

Don't miss any of the six exciting titles in
THE GARRISONS continuity, beginning in July.
Only from Silhouette Desire.

THE CEO'S SCANDALOUS AFFAIR
#1807

Available July 2007.

COMING NEXT MONTH

#333 MEN AT WORK Karen Kendall/Cindi Myers/Colleen Collins
Hot Summer Anthology
When these construction hotties pose for a charity calendar, more than a few pulses go through the roof! Add in Miami's steamy temperatures that beg a man to peel off his shirt and the result? Three sexy stories in one *very* hot collection. Don't miss it!

#334 THE ULTIMATE BITE Crystal Green
Extreme
A year ago he came to her—a vampire in need, seducing her with an incredible bite, an intimate bite…a forgettable bite? Haunted by the sensuality of that night, Kim's been searching for Stephen ever since. Imagine her surprise when she realizes he doesn't even remember her. And his surprise…when he discovers that Kim will do anything to become his Ultimate Bite…

#335 TAKEN Tori Carrington
The Bad Girls Club, Bk. 1
Seline Sanborn is a con artist. And power broker Ryder Blackwell is her handsome mark. An incredible one-night stand has Ryder falling, *hard*. But what will he do when he wakes up to find the angel in his bed gone…along with a chunk of his company's funds?

#336 THE COP Cara Summers
Tall, Dark…and Dangerously Hot! Bk. 2
Off-duty detective Nik Angelis is the first responder at a wedding-turned-murder-scene. The only witness is a fiery redhead who needs his protection—but *wants* his rock-hard body. Nik aims to be professional, but a man can take only so much….

#337 GHOSTS AND ROSES Kelley St. John
The Sexth Sense, Bk. 2
Gage Vicknair has been dreaming—incredible erotic visions—about a mysterious brown-eyed beauty. He's desperate to meet her and turn those dreams into reality. Only, he doesn't expect a ghost, a woman who was murdered, to be able to help him find her. Or that he's going to have to save the woman of his dreams from a similar fate….

#338 SHE DID A BAD, BAD THING Stephanie Bond
Million Dollar Secrets, Bk. 1
Mild-mannered makeup artist Jane Kurtz has always wished she had the nerve to go for things she wants. Like her neighbor Perry Brewer. So when she wins the lottery, she sees her chance—she's going to Vegas for the ultimate bad-girl makeover. Perry won't know what hit him. But he'll know soon. Because Perry's in Vegas, too….

www.eHarlequin.com

HBCNM0607